THE DARK HOUR

A NOVEL

ERIN LANTER

This book is a work of fiction. Characters and events
are products of the author's imagination, and any
reference to a real location or business establishment
is used fictitiously. Any resemblance to actual persons,
living or dead, or events is entirely coincidental.

THE
DARK
HOUR

*To my mom, Cindy, for nurturing in me a
love of reading and mystery, and to my dad,
Larry, who passed on his love of writing
and creativity to me. I love you both!*

1

MAMA TAUGHT ME monsters are real. They live under the bed, in the closet, and inside your head. They lurk in the darkness, waiting until you're at your weakest, then like wild animals, they come out to devour you. You can't stop them, and if you survive one, it's only a matter of time until the next one overpowers you.

Tessa James shifted uncomfortably in her chair as she waited for Dr. Raymond to call her back to his office.

How can I possibly tell that to another human being? Tessa wondered. No one, *no one*, knew what was hidden in the deepest corners of her mind, and she'd worked a lifetime to make sure it stayed that way.

She shifted again and glanced around the waiting room. It was meant to be soothing, she supposed, but the music being piped into the room and the water cascading down the tabletop fountain did nothing to calm her anxiety. It just made her have to pee.

Uncrossing and re-crossing her legs, Tessa noticed her pants clinging to the backs of her thighs. Circles darkened her shirt under her armpits. Shaking her dangling foot, she was certain she smelled of nervous sweat.

When a small man with heavy eyebrows resting above equally heavy eyeglasses appeared, she drew in a sharp breath, fighting the urge to bolt. Tessa stood and walked through the waiting room, past the fountain, and into a well-decorated office. A large, L-shaped desk dominated the right side of the room. The half dozen framed degrees, licenses, and awards hanging on the wall were a testament that someone thought he was qualified to dig into a person's most private thoughts. A small grouping of wingback chairs sat to the left. Straight ahead, a fish tank took up half the wall, the focal point from every direction.

Settling into the chair closest to the door, Tessa deposited her purse on the floor. She was sure Dr. Raymond would have a theory about why she chose that particular seat. Once she was as comfortable as she could ever be in a shrink's office, Tessa glanced up, realizing he'd been watching her. He sat with his legs crossed, an elbow propped on the arm of the chair, resting his chin on his knuckles. A typical shrink pose.

What a way to start the week, she thought.

"Ms. James, tell me what brings you in to see me today." Dr. Raymond's voice was soothing, and much deeper than she'd expected considering his slight frame.

She watched the fish swim to and fro, never making any real progress.

Just like my life, she thought.

Without taking her eyes from the fish, Tessa said, "I have a hard time trusting people, I guess."

When she turned back to him, Tessa had the feeling he could see right through her.

"You guess?" he urged. "Don't you know?"

She quickly flipped her light brown hair over her shoulder and tore her gaze away from the man who was supposed to help her. "Yes, I do. I have a hard time trusting people." She exhaled deeply. There, she'd said it.

"Can you be more specific?"

Tessa cleared her throat and scooted back in her chair. She hadn't felt this fidgety since she was a child. "People's motives for the things they say and do. I don't trust them. What are they trying to gain by being nice to me? Are they saying one thing but thinking another? I grew up believing a lot of things about people. That they are trustworthy wasn't one of them." To be more specific than that, she'd have to bust down her protective wall, something she wasn't entirely sure she was ready to do.

Dr. Raymond nodded then scribbled a note on the legal pad in his lap. He continued looking at her.

Tessa let the silence float between them for a few minutes. She wasn't being deliberately uncooperative; she just had no idea how to open up to someone else.

Pushing his glasses up the bridge of his nose with a slender index finger, Dr. Raymond said, "The first thing we need to do is dig into your beliefs about people. Then we'll see if they're really true. Healing can't truly begin until you've faced the root of your mistrust."

He made it sound so easy, but he might as well have asked her to climb Mount Everest. She looked at the clock. At least she still had thirty minutes for him to tell her where to begin.

For the next twenty-five minutes, they began to chip away at the layers, but until she felt comfortable enough to share her own vulnerabilities, she would sacrifice her mother, a woman who wasn't there to defend herself.

As the minute hand rolled toward the ten, Dr. Raymond said, "This is good."

Not really, Doc, Tessa thought. It's pretty much screwed up my entire life.

He went on. "Next time I want us to look at how your mother's beliefs and behaviors have impacted you and shaped your view of people." He glanced at his watch. "That's all the time we have for today. Next week we'll get into the hard work."

Tessa collected her purse and stood. As she turned to leave, she muttered, "Thank you."

This was going to be a long, bumpy road.

Nodding briefly at the receptionist on her way through the waiting room, Tessa was relieved. She'd ripped off the Band-Aide. It felt good to hear from someone else that the things she'd learned from Mama might be lies.

Even so, Tessa couldn't shake the feeling that she'd betrayed her mother. Despite her problems, she'd raised Tessa to be a fully functioning, albeit mistrusting, adult.

Once she was out of the building, Tessa stood on the sidewalk inhaling the scent of sunshine and car exhaust, wondering what Mama would think if she knew Tessa was planning to go looking for the monsters she'd always been warned about.

2

LAYING THE NOTES he'd taken during his session with Tessa James aside, Dr. Harold Raymond leaned forward, massaged his lower back, then settled back into his top-of-the-line, ergonomic chair. Even though the living room environment of his office made client sessions feel more relaxed, he hated sitting in the wingback chairs. Each session aggravated an old skiing injury, sending his lower back into spasm.

At sixty-eight years old, it had been years since he went down the slopes. He always felt larger than life whizzing down the snow-covered mountains, but since his injury, the adrenaline rush was just a memory.

He picked up his legal pad and read his notes from the last fifty minutes.

The first session was always the hardest. Many new clients were hesitant to share their deeply personal problems. Others didn't even know where to start.

Tessa James had both things working against her.

As a practicing clinical psychologist for more than forty

years, he'd become exceptionally skilled at nudging clients past their barriers. Tessa would require more than a nudge.

He glanced up at his fish tank, watching his finned friends swim back and forth, turning back only when they ran out of room to move forward.

How very much like life, Dr. Raymond thought, shaking his head. People only came to him when they could no longer move forward on their own.

He pulled the keyboard tray from under his desk, his fingers flew across the keys as he typed his case notes about Tessa James.

Client is a thirty-four-year-old Caucasian female. She states she's been struggling with trust issues her whole life. Her goal is to evaluate the belief that people are untrustworthy and work toward allowing herself to trust others. Client stated her mother taught her that others were dangerous and would hurt her if given the opportunity. Client deflected many personal questions, choosing mostly to speak about her mother...

Something about Tessa James troubled him. It wasn't just that she didn't trust him - why would she, considering her upbringing?

Again, he watched the fish. His eyes tracked them back and forth, the movement sparking something deep in his memory.

She seemed so familiar. Had he seen her somewhere before? He definitely remembered those eyes – an unusual shade of blue, almost turquoise like the Caribbean Sea. Even the way she narrowed them and tilted her head to the side when she listened... He was sure they'd met before.

But when?

Before the memory could fully form, his secretary buzzed

him, letting him know his next client was waiting. He'd be working late. Again.

Gathering his notepad and pen, his curiosity about Tessa James faded into the background as he prepared himself for his next session.

Looking into her psychological history would have to wait.

3

THE BUS WHEEZED to a stop. Tessa pressed her purse to her side with an elbow and inched her way forward up the steps. Three days and the mechanic still didn't know what was wrong with her car. Until he figured it out, Tessa was at the mercy of the city bus system.

As she ascended the last step, the pungent smell of public transportation filled her nose. Hot, sweaty bodies crowded together, vying for a seat near the air vent. The fatigue on the other passengers' faces made it clear they just wanted to go home and forget about the day.

After the day she'd had, that was Tessa's plan, too.

The bus lurched forward, full of sweaty sardines trying not to make eye contact with each other. That was fine by Tessa. She wasn't in the mood.

Finally, the bus reached her stop. As the door hissed open, she broke free from the crowd and began the half-mile walk from the bus stop to her front door. As she trudged down the sidewalk, her slick feet slid around in her high heels. She could already feel a blister forming on the ball of her foot. Mid-July in Kentucky wasn't the time to have to hoof it in heels.

Drenched in sweat, she finally turned up her sidewalk and slid the key into the doorknob of the small ranch-style bungalow she'd been renting for the past year. Stepping over the threshold, she kicked off her shoes, certain if she listened hard enough, she could hear them singing the "Hallelujah" chorus.

The house wasn't much to look at, but it signified her independence. After she and Drew split a year ago, her lifestyle had changed drastically. Used to living on two incomes for the better part of a decade and, rarely wanting for anything, she hadn't been prepared for the radical difference of living on her own modest salary. A news assistant didn't make much, and the money she made was all there was. It was terrifying, even if oddly liberating. Built in the 1950's, the house with its shabby decor, dated kitchen, and warped floors served as a gentle reminder that things could only get better.

Things *will* get better. Won't they? she'd wondered dozens of times since she moved in.

Tessa dropped her keys on the kitchen table and walked through the living room toward the bedroom, flexing her toes into the carpet with each step. Whoever designed business clothes didn't consider public transportation, she thought as she peeled off her slacks and the button-down shirt that had become plastered to her back. She grabbed a tank top and cotton shorts from her dresser and quickly put them on.

Her stomach growled, a reminder that she'd skipped lunch. Since she hadn't been to the grocery store in over a week, the refrigerator and pantry were bare. Staring at the almost empty shelves, she grimaced at the meager offerings, wishing the dry cereal and canned beans into a steak.

She'd resigned herself to a pack of instant oatmeal and an apple when a knock at the door stopped her hand mid-reach.

Tessa groaned.

She walked the twelve feet from the kitchen to the front door and pasted a smile on her face, ready for forced pleasantry.

Tessa bit the inside of her lip and thought, I just hope it's not Lois. The last thing she needed was a nosy neighbor talking her ear off for the next forty-five minutes about how well her rosebushes were doing despite the heat.

Why is she trying so hard to get to know me, anyway?

A glance through the peephole made her stomach clench, and the hunger pangs were quickly replaced by nausea.

4

TAKING A DEEP breath and exhaling slowly, Tessa unlocked the deadbolt and allowed the door to swing inward.

"What do you want?" she asked, turning on her heel and stalking back to the kitchen.

Following her into the kitchen, Drew said, "I thought you might be hungry. I brought Mexican food." He held up the bag of take-out like a trophy, beaming from ear to ear.

Tessa stopped mid-step. He certainly knew what she liked. Why shouldn't he? They'd been married almost ten years.

She turned to face him. His jet-black hair with flecks of gray at the temples, crystal blue eyes, and crooked smile hadn't lost their charm, even after all these years. If anything, missing him for the past year had made her appreciate them even more.

I guess it's true what they say about absence and the heart, Tessa thought.

But the pain of his abandonment was still raw.

"Is this supposed to be some kind of peace offering, Drew? Because you're a little late for that. A couple enchiladas won't make up for you walking out on me."

"What about enchiladas *and* salsa *and* guacamole?" Her anger had done nothing to dampen his megawatt smile and boyish charm.

"It's nothing to joke about," Tessa snapped.

"I know, I'm sorry," he said, looking around the small house. "I just thought you might want dinner."

It occurred to Tessa that this was the first time Drew had seen her new place. She couldn't imagine what he must have been thinking – only that it was a huge step down from what she had been used to.

"I know how strapped you've been since we split…" Drew continued.

"Since *you* split. I've been strapped since *you* split. I didn't split, remember?" Venom laced her words. It was true, though. She'd gotten used to living on a tight budget. Take-out was a rare treat.

Drew dropped the bag to his side and looked at the faded mauve carpet. "I just wanted to do something nice for you. I'll go now." He took a few steps forward and placed the bag on the kitchen table, then turned and began walking toward the door.

Tessa bit her tongue until it hurt. True, Drew had broken her heart and left her financially strapped, but he'd also tried to make the divorce as easy on her as possible. Through the entire process, he'd never said an unkind word, just wished her a lifetime of happiness. He'd also sent money for birthdays and holidays because, determined to make it without him, she'd refused alimony.

As he placed his hand on the doorknob, Tessa finally found her voice – barely above a whisper. "Please stay."

They soon fell into the routine that had become second nature during their decade long marriage. As they worked side by side – Tessa putting the food on plates and Drew getting the drinks – any observer would have thought they were still a couple.

Settling into opposite chairs at the small dining table, they clinked their forks together, a ritual they'd begun when they started dating during their first year of college.

Drew dipped a tortilla chip into the salsa and Tessa cut off a bite of enchilada. She closed her eyes and smiled as she chewed. It was delicious, a luxury she rarely allowed herself.

In two minutes, she'd devoured half the food on her plate. When she looked up, Drew was eying her curiously.

"Hungry?"

"I skipped lunch," she answered simply. He didn't need to know she'd spent her lunch break at a shrink's office.

"Do you need money for food?"

"I'm fine, really," she assured. "My car is at the mechanic, and as soon as I have transportation again, I'm going shopping."

As long as the mechanic doesn't bleed me dry, she mused.

"If you're sure…"

"Yes. Now, can you pass the guacamole?" she said, trying not to sound like a charity case.

He half smiled and slid the Styrofoam container across the table. She spooned a glob of it onto her remaining enchilada and relished the last few bites.

A few minutes later, the dishes were pushed to the middle of the table as Tessa and Drew fell into comfortable conversation. For the next half hour, they talked about family and friends, the horrors of working nine-to-five, and the temptation to run off and live in a cottage on a deserted island.

Soon, Tessa's sides hurt. Drew always had a knack for impressions and had provided countless hours of entertainment during their lean years. Tonight, he was imitating his assistant, Dorothy, a woman in her mid-fifties who had the habit of replaying conversations out loud. And there was no whispering with Dorothy. Her normal voice rivaled a foghorn.

Tessa wiped a tear from her eye and took a deep breath. "It's been a long time since I've laughed that hard."

Drew nodded slightly and took a sip of water. "Me too."

As suddenly as it had started, the carefree laughter was over. "Why are you here, Drew? After a year, there has to be a reason. Other than an overwhelming urge to bring enchiladas to your ex-wife."

Drew shrugged, almost imperceptibly, and looked toward the kitchen. "I've been thinking about you. I miss you, Tess."

Tessa looked down at her hands and asked the question she figured everyone in their situation would ask, "Where did we go wrong?"

"You didn't trust me. You didn't trust anybody. I always seemed to be hitting a wall with you. I knew you loved me the best you could, but you wouldn't let me love you back. It was almost like you were waiting for me to hurt you." Drew picked up his fork and swirled it around in the mole sauce left on his plate. "Fourteen years is a long time to live with that."

With that, Drew stood, gathered the plates, and took them to the kitchen. After placing them in the dishwasher, he walked back to the table and kissed the top of Tessa's head. "I love you, Tess. Always have." Then he was gone, the front door clicking shut behind him.

He was right. She'd been waiting for him to hurt her. Her marriage was just another casualty of her deep-seated mistrust.

"Thanks for screwing me up beyond repair, Mama," Tessa said as she stood and snapped off the kitchen light.

5

MAD AT HERSELF and mad at Drew, Tessa slipped on her sneakers and headed out the door. She needed air.

Her appointment with Dr. Raymond had thrown her off balance. It took every ounce of control she had not to think about the things she'd told him about her mother. Irrational as it may have been, Tessa felt that she'd somehow betrayed her mother by talking about her to a complete stranger. If that wasn't bad enough, that stranger was a psychologist. If she were still alive, Tessa knew her mama would hate her.

She replayed the appointment in her head as she walked through her neighborhood, her concentration broken only by the occasional laughter of children playing in their front lawns.

Was she ever that carefree?

Word by word, she remembered everything she'd said to Dr. Raymond. Her mother's inability to trust; her own inability to trust. Was it Mama's fault? She felt a pang of guilt for even entertaining the thought, but where else would a child learn that people were dangerous and waiting for an opportunity to hurt you?

Exhaling sharply Tessa forced the guilt away. After a mental shake, Tessa looked around, realizing she was on a street lined with massive homes.

Definitely not my neighborhood, Tessa thought.

Everything looked perfect. Luxury cars were parked in front of custom designed houses. Her tiny, rented bungalow paled in comparison. Even the landscaping in this neighborhood looked like it cost more than her annual salary.

At some point, she must have dreamed of having this kind of life. Didn't most people? Sadness settled in the pit of her stomach. That dream, like many others, was long dead.

The first big raindrop landed on her shoulder. Turning to go home, she took one last glance at a life she'd never have. The big house, nice car, perfect family with 2.3 children – it wasn't for her.

Half of these people have probably done time for insider trading, anyway, she reasoned.

The sky darkened quickly, looking as though daylight had almost completely given way to night. The rain fell harder now, each drop leaving a dark splotch on her purple tank top.

Just before she turned toward home, movement in the front window of the house at the end of the street caught her eye. The house, mostly hidden by an old oak tree, looked eerie, haunted. She suddenly felt uneasy.

Unsafe, a little voice in her head warned, but her feet wouldn't move.

A man had something slung over his shoulder and was struggling under its weight. Slipping behind a shrub, Tessa peered around the side. She squinted through the rain, straining to make out a form. Through the raindrops, her brain registered what she was seeing. Tessa shook her head and blinked.

It couldn't be.

The bundle was wrapped in heavy plastic sheeting. A moment later, a hand slipped from a hole in the side. Tessa leaned forward, squinting.

An invisible hand closed around her throat. She gasped for breath.

The plastic was pulled tightly against a face. Dark hair was tangled around the face of a young woman. The dark eyes were wide and staring.

Adrenaline surged through Tessa's body. She covered her mouth in a dual effort to stop herself from screaming and throwing up.

Kneeling in the soggy grass, stomach still churning, Tessa was pelted by an ever-increasing downpour.

As the man turned to leave the room, a bolt of lightning lit up the sky. His beady eyes narrowed as his gaze fixed on her. He held it for one terrifying moment before he backed quickly out of the room.

The lights in the house went out, leaving Tessa to wonder if her mind was playing tricks on her the way Mama's did, and if it wasn't, what had she just gotten herself into?

6

THE GOLDEN SKY darkened behind him as Drew pulled into the driveway of the house he'd once shared with Tessa. Filing for divorce had been the most difficult decision he'd ever made. He had hoped it would be a wake-up call for her, a sign that she needed to stop shutting him out. Instead, she'd built an even bigger wall between them.

"I knew I couldn't trust you, and you've just proved me right," she'd said.

A year later, the words still stung. He'd known from the time they met she was carrying heavy baggage. Like an idiot, he always thought if he loved her enough, it would make everything better. Instead, he'd given all he had for fourteen years and when it was over, all she had to say was that she'd been right not to trust him.

Drew unclipped his seat belt and got out of the car, slamming the door a little too hard as he turned toward the mid-size house. A blast of cool air greeted him as he stepped into the house just as it began to rain. He wiped his feet on the rug inside the front door.

Traces of Tessa still lingered everywhere. When she moved out, she left most of the things she'd used to decorate. On the mantel over the fireplace was a painting they'd bought on their honeymoon. The artist had beautifully captured the crystal blue water of the Caribbean and the orange sun setting over a grove of palm trees. They loved the Caribbean and would sometimes dream about selling everything to pull up stakes and move there.

Now that day would never come.

She hadn't wanted to take the painting, and he couldn't look at it without the familiar ache twisting in his gut. But he couldn't bring himself to take it down, either.

The day she moved her stuff out, she hadn't shed a tear. Not Tessa. The walls she'd built around herself were waterproof. Even though she'd known it would be a struggle to make ends meet on her salary and had basically no support system, she'd walked out of the house with her chin held high.

I, on the other hand, Drew thought, have felt guilty every day since then. Yes, I hurt her, but I also realized too late that I had the resources to handle sudden singleness better than she did.

After seeing Tessa tonight, the guilt was even heavier. It wasn't just the shabby house. As a stockbroker, he'd always been the money-maker. He knew she wouldn't be able to afford the life she was accustomed to on only her income.

But tonight, it was something else. Some of her spark was gone.

"What did I do to her?" he mumbled as he walked to the fridge to grab a beer.

As he popped the lid off the bottle, his cell phone rang. He took a quick gulp, then set the bottle down and crossed the kitchen to pick up his phone.

"Hello?" His voice was gruff.

"Drew, baby, what's the matter?" the female voice on the other end purred.

"Oh, hi, Camille," he said, almost choking on the words. "Nothing."

"Now, don't give me that," she said sweetly. "I know you well enough by now to know when you're upset."

He winced and rubbed his temple with his free hand. After almost a year of watching him mope about Tessa, his friend Pete had set him up with a girl he promised would be a lot of fun and who wouldn't try to keep him at arm's length.

That had been an understatement. Camille was a partier and probably the clingiest girl he'd ever met. Too clingy.

Drew frowned.

"Hello-o?" Camille sang. "You still there?"

The corner of Drew's mouth twitched. "Sorry, I'm still here." *I am sorry I'm here*, Drew thought, then added, "It's just been a rough day."

"I'm so sorry, darling. Want me to come over?"

"No," Drew answered too quickly. "I'm just going to watch some TV and go to bed. I'm afraid I wouldn't be much fun."

"Okay, then. I'll call you in the morning to see how you're feeling, alright?"

"Sure. Goodnight." He disconnected the call and retrieved the bottle he'd left on the counter.

She's probably the worst rebound girlfriend ever, he thought, then immediately felt guilty. Pete had been right. Camille was a lot of fun, and it really had been a nice change to be in a relationship with someone who wasn't always on the defensive. He never had to wonder where he stood with Camille. She thought he hung the moon.

He slammed the bottle back on the counter. But I didn't hang the moon. I walked out on my wife and left her less trusting than when I found her. And even though it has been a relief to be with someone so open and caring, she's not what I want, he admitted to himself.

He wanted someone who wasn't going to be dependent on him, someone who wouldn't be completely devastated if he wasn't around, and someone who could pull herself up by her bootstraps and get on with her life.

He wanted Tessa.

But she would never give him another chance.

Drew chugged the last of the beer and tossed the bottle into the recycling bin. The corner of his mouth drooped. Tessa had always been on him to recycle his bottles. Until she came along, he'd never even thought about it. When they were still together, somehow he'd missed that her reminders had been her own way of showing him she cared.

Shaking his head, he walked upstairs, changed his clothes, and looked at the clock.

Seven-thirty. He climbed into bed and clicked on the TV. It was too early to sleep. And tonight, he thought, I probably won't be able to sleep anyway.

7

A TENDRIL OF fear slithered around Tessa's spine, squeezing her chest. Her breath came out in short, labored bursts. Blood pounded in her ears.

She couldn't stop shaking; her only thought was that she had been seen.

Was that monster going to come for her?

I have to get out of here, she thought frantically, eyes darting around.

Rising on unsteady legs, Tessa moved quickly toward the nearest house and pounded on the front door. "Please!" The cry escaped her throat in a constricted whisper. "Somebody!"

The windows of the house behind the oak tree had been dark for several minutes, but that didn't mean he wouldn't be back, that he wouldn't come after her.

The rain was still coming down in steady sheets. Desperately wanting to shield herself from the pounding drops and her own vulnerability, she climbed between the hedges and the cold stone exterior of the expansive home. She crouched down, pulling her legs close and wrapping her arms around them, trying to make herself invisible. Burying her face between her knees, she clamped her eyes shut against the image that kept replaying in her mind.

As the rain tapered off into a light drizzle, she unfolded herself and raised her head just enough to scan the street.

The light came on in the house behind the tree. The front door opened.

Run! her brain screamed.

She darted from behind the hedges and ran through the shadows until she reached her own front door. Slipping inside, she flipped the lock and deadbolt into place, and leaned against the door, her breath shallow and ragged.

Questions pounded in her head. Was she safe? Had the man followed her? Had she really seen what she thought she saw?

It wouldn't be the first time her mind had played tricks on her.

She picked her cell phone up off the kitchen counter and scrolled through her contacts, selecting a number she knew by heart.

As the phone rang, she glanced at the clock. It was only eight-thirty. How was it possible she'd only been gone an hour and a half?

"Hello?" Drew sounded cautious.

Tessa bit her quivering lip. "Can you come over?" Even to her own ears, her voice sounded strained.

"What's wrong?"

"I just – "

"Tessa. Tell me what's wrong," Drew demanded.

"I just – "

"I'll be right over." The line went dead.

A knock at the door pulled her from her daze. She realized she hadn't moved since she called Drew.

Walking quickly toward the door, she suddenly slowed her pace. Was it really Drew, or had the man followed her, planning to make sure she could never tell anyone what she saw? It was almost as if her mother's voice was whispering to her.

Taking a deep breath, Tessa closed the distance between herself and the door. A glance through the peephole showed Drew standing on the other side, shifting anxiously from one leg to the other. Just as he raised his hand to knock again, Tessa unlocked the door and jerked it open.

Drew's eyes widened. "What happened?"

She turned and led him into her small living room. As she passed the mirror in the short hallway, her own reflection startled her. Her light brown hair hung in strings and lay plastered against her face and neck. Her blue eyes looked like ice against her pale face.

She drew in a shuddering breath.

Drew noticed and came within a few inches of her. He grasped her arms and moved his hands up and down her shoulders, trying to warm her. "I want you to put on some dry clothes," he ordered. "I'm going to make a pot of coffee, then you're going to tell me what happened."

Tessa nodded and silently obeyed.

When she emerged from the bedroom, dry but still chilled to the bone, Drew handed her a cup of coffee and motioned for her to sit on the sofa. He covered her lap with a blanket and settled in next to her.

She took a sip, then eyed the coffee suspiciously.

"It's decaf," he offered.

"I hate decaf," she protested weakly, then took another sip. Why was decaf in her pantry, anyway?

"The last thing you need right now is caffeine. You already look like you're about to jump out of your skin."

They sat in silence for several minutes as Tessa allowed the hot liquid to warm her.

"Tell me what happened," Drew urged softly as Tessa lowered the mug to her lap.

"I know this is a terrible inconvenience for you. I just didn't know who else to call…"

"Tessa, you look like you've just been put through the wringer. Tell me what's going on," Drew demanded.

She raised the mug to her lips and took another sip of coffee. "I was taking a walk. I must not have been paying attention to where I was going, because I ended up in The Estates."

Drew waited for her to continue.

"I had a pretty rough day and needed to clear my head. It started raining…" She paused for another sip.

"That explains why you were completely drenched, but not why you're so spooked."

Taking a deep, shaky breath, she continued, "I was getting ready to turn around and start home when the first raindrops started. But then I saw something that stopped me."

She looked into her mug, now almost empty, trying to shake the image. She brought the cup to her lips and drained the rest of the coffee. Desperately wanting a refill, she hoped Drew would take the hint.

He didn't. Instead, he pressed, "What did you see?"

After another shuddering breath, Tessa forced the words out. "I saw a man in the window of a house. The house gave me the creeps for some reason. It didn't look like it belonged in The Estates. Anyway, the man was carrying something. It was wrapped in plastic sheeting and he was having a hard time with it. It looked heavy."

"Go on," Drew urged, never taking his eyes from Tessa's face.

"Part of the plastic slipped open, and I saw a hand. A hand slipped through the opening." Tessa was surprised how calm she sounded.

I must be in shock, she thought.

"A hand?"

Tessa ran her fingers through her still damp hair. Of course Drew would have a hard time believing her. Who wouldn't? The south was all horse farms, bourbon, and manners, not murders in quiet, upscale neighborhoods. "Yes, a hand," she insisted. "While he struggled with it, the plastic pulled tight and I saw a face." Her calm was beginning to scare her. Only a sociopath wouldn't feel anything about what she'd just seen.

Drew cocked an eyebrow. "You think he was carrying a body wrapped in plastic through his house?"

"Yes, I do."

Tessa listened to the nighttime sounds of her house. Traffic in the distance, a ticking clock, the ice maker in the freezer kicking on. It seemed so… normal.

"Are you sure?" Drew asked. "I mean, you're sure you saw this? It wouldn't be the first time – "

Clenching her jaw, Tessa said, "I saw it, Drew. And not just that. I think he saw me, too."

Drew leaned back on the sofa. His eyebrows furrowed the way they always did that when he was thinking. "Are you telling me that you think this man murdered someone, and that he might have seen you?"

Tessa nodded. The shock was wearing off. Panic zipped through her stomach. Her heart hammered inside her chest. "Yes." Glancing at her hand, still holding the empty mug, she noticed it was shaking.

A look that mirrored her own flitted across Drew's face. "You have to go to the police, Tess."

Her stomach sank. She'd been down this road before.

8

HE RAN HIS hand across his forehead as rain and sweat dripped into his eyes. The evening hadn't gone as he'd planned.

He cursed himself for his carelessness. How could he have let himself be seen?

What were the odds that someone would look through his window at the exact moment he was moving her? Who would be outside in a torrential downpour? Who could see past the giant oak that blocked most of his house?

Apparently at least one person, who he would have to make sure he dealt with.

The wipers moved back and forth across the windshield in a futile attempt to clear the deluge coming from the sky. This rain was certainly causing problems. He'd known there was a chance, but even the meteorologists hadn't seen this one coming. His plans would have to be adjusted, and he'd have to come up with another place to stash the body. Everything could have been perfect; he could have been in the clear and she would have never even been missed.

When someone is practically knocking on death's door,

no one asks questions. Family and friends are expecting it, so no one causes a fuss when they die. There are tears, a funeral, and finally, acceptance. Everyone moves on with only "what a shame" whenever the deceased's name is mentioned.

After almost an hour of driving, he still didn't know what to do. The woman who'd seen him would have probably already gone to the police. They'd come knocking on his door any minute.

He glanced at the clock on the dashboard. The glowing numbers told him he was running out of time. It was a quarter of eight. Night shift awaited, and he had to be calm enough not to raise any questions from his coworkers.

A smile played on his lips when he realized he had the perfect hiding place. No one would even think to question him if they found her.

For the first time in an hour, his heart rate slowed, and a sense of calm washed over him.

It would all be okay.

9

LOIS SIMMONS PLACED a plate of sliced meatloaf on the kitchen table and settled her thick frame into the chair. Her husband, Walter, was already helping himself to generous portions of mashed potatoes and green beans.

"Did you work up an appetite today, honey?" she asked her husband from across the table.

"Yep," Walter grunted as he shoveled food into his mouth. After working a twelve-hour shift as a hospital custodian, he was rarely in the mood for conversation until after dinner and a drink, usually bourbon.

Lois looked over her shoulder and out the window toward their neighbor's house. "The woman next door had a visitor tonight. Twice in one night, actually." Her eyes snapped with excitement.

"Is that so?"

"Yes! And what a nice-looking man he is! I've always thought she's such a pretty girl, and it's a shame she never has anyone over. Don't you think she must have a very lonely life?"

Lois asked, piling food onto her own plate. Lois never let her full figure keep her from enjoying a home-cooked meal.

"I wouldn't know," Walt said, noncommittal. "If she's alone, it's probably because she wants to be, dear. She has a right to her privacy."

Lois scooped a generous bite of meatloaf and mashed potatoes onto her fork and relished the flavor. She'd decided years ago that since she was in her fifties, she was entitled to a few extra inches around her waist. She never understood women who watched every morsel they put in their mouths. Life was to be enjoyed, Lois reasoned, and how could they possibly enjoy life when they were nibbling on lettuce and sprouts all the time?

"Why would anyone *choose* to be alone?" Lois asked, incredulously, spearing a green bean and popping it into her mouth.

A shrug was Walt's only response.

Lois leaned back in her chair. She knew what her husband thought of her: the neighborhood busybody who knew almost everything about their neighbors' personal lives. She never considered herself nosy, only observant and well-informed. It wasn't her fault she saw everything that happened on their street while she was in her kitchen running her home-based bakery.

When it came to this particular neighbor, though, she'd been miffed more than once when her friendly offerings of muffins or cookies went unacknowledged. It drove Lois crazy. After all, she'd fumed to her long-suffering husband many times, anyone with any kind of manners would have at least dropped a thank you note in the mailbox. The note never came, though, and Lois couldn't let it go.

"Aren't you even a little curious about what's going on with her? She's never outside, except when she's mowing her grass, and she doesn't make any effort to get to know us or any of the other neighbors. But having the same handsome man visit her twice in one night – don't you think that means something?"

Walt dropped his napkin in his lap and rested a hand on the table. "Lois, whatever is going on with that woman is none of your business. You've got to pry yourself away from the windows and stop spying on her," he chastised.

"Spy? I'm not spying, Walter," she said as though she were addressing a child. "It just so happens that I spend a lot of time in the kitchen, and the window over the sink gives me a perfect view of the front of her house. Lois's Loaves is really starting to take off." Lois paused and proudly patted her short, ash blond hair. "It's not my fault if I've noticed over the past year that nobody but her ever seems to be coming or going."

"Whatever you say, Lois," Walt said, picking his fork back up and shoveling in a mouthful of mashed potatoes.

"Maybe she just needs a friend," Lois commented, more to herself than to Walt, who seemed to be tuning her out. She snapped her fingers. "I'll take her one of my cream cheese pound cakes. Nobody can resist those."

Walt scraped up the last bite of food from his plate, then announced, "I'm going to watch TV." He stood, the legs of the chair scraping the faded linoleum as he pushed it back.

Lois didn't seem to notice.

She tapped a short pink fingernail on the scratched table and furrowed her brow. "Let's see," she mumbled. "I've got orders the next couple days, so I won't have time to bake anything extra." She placed her index finger on her lips, an unconscious gesture she made when she was deep in thought. "I can take it over Friday. If she's lucky, she'll have someone to share it with. "Now, what's her name again?" Her finger went back to her lips. Lois thought several moments before it came to her. "Ah. I think it's Tessa something."

10

DREW SANK ONTO the sofa and leaned his head back. Of all the ways he thought he might spend this evening, sitting in Tessa's living room while she told him an almost unbelievable story about someone carrying a dead woman wrapped in plastic would never have crossed his mind.

It had been a struggle to keep his mind from wandering to the most logical place. It wouldn't be the first time Tessa thought she saw something that didn't really happen.

Ever since her mom died a couple years ago, Tessa hadn't been the same. At first he just assumed it came from not knowing what to do without having to take care of her mom, but it seemed to go a little deeper. More than once, he'd been afraid the trauma of finding her body had pushed Tessa into some kind of psychological break. He was no expert on the subject, but he knew enough to be concerned.

Now, with the help of a sleeping pill, Tessa was asleep, leaving Drew to wonder if it was possible that her biggest fear was coming true – that the monsters that lived in her mother's head had found their way into Tessa's.

11

LIGHT FILTERED THROUGH the bedroom window and lay in streaks across the bed. Tuesday morning. Tessa groaned and buried her face in the pillow. Drew had insisted she take a sleeping pill last night, and she'd been too upset and exhausted to argue. Now she felt foggy.

Bit by bit, images from the night before formed in her mind. Walking for what seemed like hours, rain, Drew's concerned face.

Her gut clenched.

She'd seen a man carrying a woman who was wrapped in plastic. Their eyes had met.

Those eyes. Why were they bothering her?

Tessa's pulse quickened and she sat straight up in bed. Suddenly restless, she got up, walked quickly to the bathroom, and leaned over the sink, clasping the edge to steady herself against the lingering drowsiness. She turned on the faucet and splashed cold water on her face. When she raised her head, she noticed a note taped to the mirror.

Tessa, I slept on the couch last night. You'll find the blanket and pillow where I left them. I had an early meeting and had to go home before you woke up. A rental car has been delivered so you don't have to take the bus. The key is on the kitchen table. Come straight home after work. I'll be here with you.

Drew

P.S. I know you don't feel like you can trust your own mind right now, but please go to the police station this morning to report what you saw. If you don't, I will.

Leaning over the sink, Tessa examined her face in the mirror. Dark circles rested beneath each puffy eye. Lines creased her forehead. She looked about ten years older than she had at this time yesterday.

Yesterday. Looking back, things had been so simple a day ago. She got up, went to work, met with Dr. Raymond, and came home. To think, only twenty-four hours ago the worst thing she had to do was talk to a shrink.

She knew what she had to do now and dreaded it.

After a quick shower and a thick layer of concealer under her eyes, she got dressed, grabbed her purse, and headed out the door, grateful that Drew had gotten her a rental. The last thing she needed right now was to be crammed into public transportation with a bunch of people who may or may not be watching her, trying to figure out why she looked so spooked.

Once in the car, she dialed her boss's number at the news station. No answer, as usual.

"Hey, Jack," she told his answering machine. "I've got an errand to run this morning, so I'll be in late. Call my cell if you need me."

Now, as long as he didn't pry into what errand she had to run, she might make it through the day without completely unraveling.

She'd tossed and turned until midnight, fighting the memories that swirled around in her head. Most of them included her mother, a sick woman who had taken Tessa down with her. Restless despite the sleeping pill, she'd finally drifted off to sleep to the image of the young woman she guessed met a tragic end last night.

Throughout the night, dreams of Mama interrupted her fitful sleep. The image she'd never been able to shake danced around in her unconscious mind: Mama, feet dangling over the second-floor banister with a cord twisted around her neck. Mama, whose monsters had gotten too big for her, had finally used her own hands to finish them off.

The dreams were nothing new. For months after Mama's suicide, Tessa would wake up in the middle of the night, drenched in sweat.

This time, though, the body of a young woman wrapped in plastic was on the floor under Mama's feet.

12

TESSA'S HANDS SHOOK as she guided the rental car into the parking spot at the police station. The only other time she'd ever been involved with the police was when she called 911 after she'd found her mom hanging from the stair railing.

Her mother's psychiatric history had been more than enough to convince the police she'd committed suicide. No questions, just condolences.

But Tessa had had questions, and the police officer at the scene went out of his way to assure her he saw this kind of thing all the time. "No doubt about it," he'd said, "this is a suicide."

Even so…

Tessa shook her head fiercely. Now was not the time to wander down that path.

As she opened the door of the police station, a whoosh of artificially cooled air greeted her. Normally it would have been a relief from the already scorching heat, but this morning it just chilled her.

The smell of stale coffee hung in the air; the walls were a

dingy white. It reminded her of the institution Mama had been in a few months before she died.

The desk sergeant, only a little smaller than a linebacker, looked up from her computer. Though her size was intimidating, her ready smile and warm brown eyes were instantly comforting. Tessa's anxiety lessened a bit.

"What can I do for you?" she asked, her speech slightly accented.

Spanish, maybe? Or Portuguese? Tessa wondered.

Shifting her purse from one shoulder to the other, Tessa wrapped her arms around her waist. She didn't know if she was shivering because she was cold or because she was nervous. "I need to report a crime," she said. Her voice was tight.

The woman nodded and motioned toward a plastic chair on the wall opposite her desk.

Tessa sat, the cold plastic biting through her slacks. Goose bumps covered her arms. She rubbed them vigorously in a vain attempt to warm herself.

Glancing around the reception area, she noticed the name plate on the sergeant's desk – Maria Ramirez. Probably Spanish after all.

On Sergeant Ramirez's desk next to her name plate was a small potted plant, a lone bit of life standing out in the dreary space.

After fifteen minutes of listening to the tick of the clock and the clicking of Sergeant Ramirez's keyboard, a broad-shouldered detective with a barrel chest appeared.

He extended his hand. "Detective Al Jefferson. Follow me." The detective's voice matched his size.

Tessa returned his handshake, then followed him between rows of desks until they reached one in the far left corner of the room. If she'd thought the front area of the police station was drab, it was nothing compared to what she was looking at now. Rows of desks that must have been at least thirty years old were covered in stacks of paper and occupied by underpaid and exhausted-looking public servants. Cracked vinyl chairs sat in front of each desk.

And I thought my cubicle was bad, Tessa thought, then immediately dismissed it. She was thankful for the police. Seeing their cars parked at houses near hers always gave her a sense of safety, knowing that if she needed them, they were only a few houses down.

Detective Jefferson motioned toward the chair in front of his desk as he lowered himself into his own chair. The vinyl squeaked as Tessa sat down.

"What can I do for you?" Detective Jefferson asked, making a futile attempt to shuffle the papers on his desk into a tidy pile.

She took a deep breath. Her mouth wouldn't form the words.

What if he doesn't take you seriously, like that other cop when you tried to tell him about Mama? her brained warned.

She clenched her jaw. Just spit it out.

"I was taking a walk last night when it started raining," she began after she'd had a moment to gather her thoughts. "As I was about to turn around to go home, I saw movement through the window of one of the houses."

The detective nodded in encouragement.

Tessa took another deep breath. This was the part that could make her look crazy if he didn't believe her, but she forged on. "I saw someone carrying a heavy bundle over his shoulder. It was wrapped in plastic. Through the plastic I saw a face."

Atta girl, she thought. You did it. It came out high-pitched and shaky, but you got the words out.

Now that the weight was off her, she really looked at Detective Jefferson for the first time since she sat down. His raised eyebrows made his tanned forehead wrinkle.

He grabbed a notepad and pen from the top drawer of his desk and started jotting down notes. Finally, his pen went still, poised above the paper. He looked up at her. "Where did you see this?"

"The Estates."

He whistled through the small gap between his front teeth. "We don't get many reports about anything going on there. The occasional robbery, but that's all. I don't think we've ever gotten a report of a dead body before."

"Sorry to be the one to break that streak," Tessa said, attempting lighthearted banter, "but I saw someone carrying the body of a woman over his shoulder."

"It was a woman?" Detective Jefferson asked as he scratched something onto the notepad.

Tessa sniffed. "Not *it*, Detective. She."

"Yes, of course. She," he repeated absently. "Can you describe her?"

"I think she had dark hair, and from what I could tell she looked fairly young. It looked like she had dark eyes, but I can't be sure since it was raining so hard and her face was completely pale." Tessa's words were clipped. Something about this detective rubbed her the wrong way. Maybe it was that he'd referred to that poor woman as "it." Maybe it was nothing and her nerves were just raw.

"Do you know the address?" Detective Jefferson asked, his voice softer as though he noticed her frustration.

The vinyl chair squeaked as Tessa shifted. "I didn't see the house number, but it was at the end of the street, hidden by a big tree. The house wasn't falling apart or anything, but it looked like it wasn't as well-maintained as the other houses on the street."

Detective Jefferson scratched more notes onto his pad, then without even looking up asked, "Did you get a good look at the man?"

Tessa shivered. "Yes, I did."

"Describe him, please." His pen still hovered just above the paper.

"He wasn't tall, but not short either. Maybe around five feet ten or eleven. He was thin, but not skinny. Pretty average from what I could tell, but I saw his eyes, and they didn't look right. They looked… dead."

The pen stopped writing and the detective looked up. "Did he see you?"

Tessa shrugged. "Maybe. He looked in my direction."

"Did you get the impression that he saw you?" he asked, slowly this time.

Again, Tessa shrugged.

Detective Jefferson studied Tessa for several long moments before dropping his eyes back to his notepad. "Let me double-check to make sure I've got this straight. Last night you were taking a walk in The Estates and saw a man carrying a young woman who was wrapped in plastic over his shoulder. You don't know the address, but the house looked creepy and was mostly hidden by a tree. You saw his eyes but aren't sure if he saw you or not. Is that correct?"

"Yes."

"But this man *might* have seen you?"

"It's possible, yes," Tessa said, fighting to keep her voice level. "The problem is, I'm having a hard time being certain if I really saw this."

He dropped his pen onto his desk and brought his fingertips to a point under his chin. "Are you married, Ms. James?"

"No."

"Do you live with anyone?"

"No." Tessa's shoulders drooped.

"Have you told anyone about this?"

"Just my ex-husband."

"What does he think about it? Does he think you really saw it?"

Tessa sighed. "I wouldn't know. I should tell you that there was one other time I thought I saw a crime, but it turned out I was mistaken."

The detective pursed his lips and said, "I see."

"Can I go now?" Tessa asked, heat creeping up her neck.

"Yes." He opened the top drawer of his desk and pulled out a business card. "We'll take a drive through The Estates and see if we notice anything." Extending the card across his desk, he said, "Feel free to call if you think of anything that could be useful."

Implying I'm not useful now, she thought.

Tessa nodded and stood, silently making her way out of the police station.

Detective Jefferson had been kind, and that almost made the embarrassment worse. If only she could be sure of what she saw, then she could assure herself that it wasn't happening again.

13

WHEN SHE FINALLY arrived at work, Tessa was met with concern. Minutes after she settled into her cubicle, she looked up to find her boss, Jack Stein, leaning on top of the make-shift wall.

"Everything okay?" he asked, eyebrows arched in worry.

"Yes," Tessa lied. "Everything is fine."

The eyebrows furrowed. "You sure? Being late for work isn't like you."

Spinning her chair slightly toward him, she looked at the creases on his forehead. He seemed genuinely concerned for her well-being. She smiled. "Yes, Jack. Everything is just fine." Somehow, in that moment, looking into the face of someone who cared about her, everything did seem fine.

He let a couple beats pass. "If all is well…" He slapped the top of the cubicle wall, turned, and walked toward his office.

All is well, indeed, Tessa thought. Thanks to the paranoia I inherited from Mama, I feel like I'm walking around with a target on my back.

She shook her head to clear her mind of those cold, dead

eyes. Then, clenching her teeth, she focused on her work. There was a pile of rewrites in her inbox and they wouldn't take care of themselves. She got into the rhythm, her concentration broken only by the sound of other news assistants tapping on their keyboards and phones ringing in the distance. She took a break to stretch and glanced at her clock. It was ten after five. Somehow, she'd managed to work through the entire pile of articles that had been waiting for her attention.

Rubbing the back of her neck, Tessa realized she'd been at it for six hours straight, not even noticing her growing hunger. It had been a long time since Tessa lost track of time like that.

Gathering the stack of rewritten articles, she dropped them in the box outside Jack's office, then went back to her desk to gather her things. Absently waving at her coworkers still seated at their desks, she walked out into the blistering summer heat and crossed the parking lot to the rental car.

Hoping she'd have a little time alone before Drew got to her house, she quickly backed out of the parking lot and eased into the rush hour traffic.

A half hour later, she pulled into her driveway with the nagging worry about how she'd lost track of time.

With the way this week had been so far, she had more to tell Dr. Raymond at her next appointment than either of them bargained for.

14

THE SUN WOULD be setting soon, and he was desperate to get a look at the houses in this neighborhood before dark. She'd been taking a walk that night, which meant she had to live relatively close to his neighborhood.

Early this morning, after his shift was over, he'd driven through the surrounding neighborhoods, determined to figure out where the woman lived. He needed to know. His survival depended on finding her, but the streets here were poorly lit. He could make out little more than silhouettes of houses, standing neatly in a row like little soldiers.

He hadn't been thinking last night. Now there was a possible witness to his blunder. But maybe, if he could find her, the problem could be taken care of. He had to find her tonight. He wouldn't feel calm until he did.

He passed moderately sized houses, nice in their own way but not suited to his taste. A few children were playing outside, many of them being called in for the night as he drove by.

Finally, he found himself on a street lined with small,

ranch-style homes. Toys were strewn across the lawns; bikes lay haphazardly on the sidewalks.

He supposed she could have walked from here, but it wasn't likely. Still, he couldn't rule it out. He slowed as a car that looked a bit too nice for this neighborhood pulled into a driveway. A man with dark hair got out carrying a pizza.

He shook his head. That guy should watch out, he thought. Somebody might try to break into a car like that around here.

The realization that a luxury car would stick out on this street made him press his foot a little harder on the gas pedal. His would definitely be noticed.

Sweat moistened his palms as a patrol car rolled slowly down the street. He had to get out of here.

Just as he turned around to head home, he glanced through the window of the house the car had just pulled up to and saw the face of the woman that could be his undoing.

A smile touched his lips. "Gotcha," he whispered, an almost euphoric feeling washing over him. Making a mental note of the address, he pressed the accelerator and breathed a sigh of relief when he finally pulled into his garage.

He'd found her. The situation was under his control. He would erase the threat, and this time, he'd make sure there were no witnesses.

15

DREW'S CAR WASN'T in the driveway, so Tessa quickly unlocked the front door and went in. She held her breath, straining to hear anything amiss in the silence. Exhaling the air she'd been holding in her lungs, she dropped her keys and purse on the kitchen table as she passed.

Minutes later, she was wearing shorts and a T-shirt. Flexing her toes in the thin carpet, she walked to the kitchen for a glass of water. As she drank, a knock at the door made her pause. She tensed.

"Who is it?" she called, her voice a few octaves too high. She didn't take a single step toward the door.

"Drew."

She set her glass on the counter and walked down the short hall toward the front door. She opened it to find Drew standing there with a pizza and a six-pack of Mountain Dew. "I brought dinner," he said, stepping into the house.

Tessa turned and walked back toward the kitchen. "Twice in two evenings. A girl could get used to this."

"I could, too," Drew offered as he followed her. "How are you?"

Tessa shrugged. "Fine."

Sliding the pizza onto the counter, he said, "Are you seriously trying to make me believe that? I was here last night. Remember? I saw how scared you were." He put the Mountain Dew next to the pizza and turned to face her. "How are you really?"

She sighed. "Still breathing, so I've got that going for me."

He nodded. "How'd it go at the police station?"

She narrowed her eyes. "How did you know I went?"

Drew raised one shoulder and let it drop. He smirked and shifted his eyes away from her. "Because you wouldn't want me to do it for you, and you knew I would. That, and there's no way you'd allow someone's death to go unnoticed."

"Right on both accounts," Tessa admitted. "The detective I talked to was nice enough. I felt bad reporting something I'm not even sure happened."

"I know, but don't you think it's better to report something and be wrong than keep it to yourself when a murder occurred?"

"I suppose. He gave me his card in case I remember anything else."

"That's something. At least he didn't dismiss you as a nutcase." Drew visibly winced. "Sorry. You know what I meant."

Tessa nodded. "That's something, I guess. Still, I'm worried. How long would it take for someone to break in here, kill me, and leave without anyone ever noticing? Ten minutes, tops?"

"Don't think like that," Drew admonished. "That guy doesn't even know where you live."

"How can I *not* think like that? It's a possibility." Tessa visibly shuddered. "Anyway, let's eat. I missed lunch."

"Again? Tessa, you've got to – "

"I know, I know. I need to take care of myself. By the time I got to work there was a mountain of things I had to rewrite. I just lost track of time," Tessa defended. "Besides, I didn't have much of an appetite."

Reaching into the cabinet, she took out plates and a glass for Drew. Dumping the rest of her water in the sink, she popped the tab of one of the soda cans and poured it in. Drew put two slices of veggie deluxe pizza on each plate. Once again, they'd fallen into the comfortable routine they'd had for years.

It felt good to have that stability again, but she didn't want to need him. The truth was, though, right now she did need him. If a killer might be looking for her, she didn't want to let Drew out of her sight.

As they carried their dinner into the living room, the irony of how her life had turned out struck her. She'd spent their whole marriage keeping Drew at arm's length, and now that they were divorced, she found herself in a situation that made her desperate to keep him close.

Although, to her knowledge, while they were married there wasn't anyone who would want to kill her. A smile tugged at the corner of her mouth. Looking back on some of their arguments, she was sure Drew must have entertained the idea from time to time.

Drew was already squatting in front of the DVD player when she came into the living room. He stood, then settled in next to her on the sofa, clicking on the TV with the remote. As they ate, they watched a comedy about a husband and wife who were trying to come up with new, and often hilarious, ways to kill each other to avoid losing half of everything to the other in a divorce.

Later, as Tessa drifted off to sleep, she had the impression of Drew leaning over her, covering her with a blanket, leaving the scent of his aftershave behind.

She slept soundly, waking Wednesday morning to the sound of birds chirping and the sun shining through the bay window in the living room.

Throwing back the blanket, she yawned and arched her back to loosen her spine. As she walked to the bathroom, she realized there was no sign of Drew.

Did he already leave? she wondered. What time is it?

She walked into the bathroom and froze. The sun shone through the long, narrow window over the shower, leaving her no need to turn on the light. On the wall, next to the shower, was a smear of blood.

Please God, no.

Where is Drew?

She took a step closer. Her mouth went dry. Something was dripping.

Hand shaking, she braced herself for what she might find. Grasping the shower curtain, she jerked it back quickly, a scream getting caught in her throat.

16

"HEY, I'M NAKED in here!" Drew shouted. "Why are you screaming at me?"

Tessa grabbed a towel off the bar next to the shower and threw it at him.

"There's no need for violence," he teased as he wrapped the towel around his waist.

"You almost gave me a heart attack," she growled through clenched teeth. "What are you doing in here?"

Drew held the towel closed with one hand and waved around the shower with the other one. "Isn't it obvious?"

Hands on her hips, Tessa glared at him.

"Okay, look," Drew said, stepping out of the shower, still dripping wet from the waist up. "You fell asleep on the couch during the movie. I didn't want to wake you, so I slept in your bed. I hope that's okay." He ran his free hand through his hair, trying to get the excess water out.

"Why wouldn't it be?" she snapped. "You used to sleep in my bed all the time." She turned on her heel and stalked out of the bathroom, angry at Drew for scaring her and angry at herself for letting her mind go to the worst possible scenario. For a moment, she'd actually believed she would find Drew's mutilated body when she opened the shower curtain. That fear had been replaced with rage.

Several minutes later, Drew emerged from the bathroom, smelling like her lavender shampoo and wearing his clothes from the night before. "I came straight from work last night and didn't pack a bag, so I need to go home to change before work."

"Fine," Tessa said simply. Her hair was a knotted mess that she'd managed to pull back into a ponytail while Drew finished grooming himself. Even in his dirty clothes, he looked impeccable. She, on the other hand, was a mess.

He smiled as he passed her – too closely – and walked into the kitchen. "Got any juice?" he asked, peering into the refrigerator.

"No," she snapped.

"Are you already sick of having me around? I'm surprised our marriage lasted a full ten years."

"It's not that, Drew," she said, reaching for a coffee mug. The truth was, she didn't know why she was upset – other than the fact that he'd just scared a decade off her lifespan.

He closed the refrigerator door. "Then what? I'm just trying to help you, Tess. Have I done something wrong?"

She slammed the mug on the warped Formica countertop and turned toward him, her face hot with anger. "No, Drew, you haven't done something wrong. You just left me, that's all. And now that I'm having a tough time, you just waltz back into my life like some knight in shining armor. But I can't do this. I can't play house knowing it's not going to last."

Eyes wide, Drew studied at her, then dropped his eyes to

the floor. When he looked up, they were filled with sadness. Maybe regret. She couldn't tell.

Closing the distance between them, Drew put his arms around her and rested his chin on her head. She stiffened. She'd forgotten how safe she felt when he hugged her.

Refusing to allow herself to get comfortable in it, she stepped out of his embrace. "I'm not some damsel in distress."

His eyes searched her face. "I miss you, Tess. The last few days made me remember what it was like when we were together. We had fun. We were good together. Maybe we could be again."

She unconsciously crossed her arms over her chest, instinctively trying to protect herself. Her own steely gaze met his pleading eyes. "I'm seeing a shrink. What more do you want from me?"

Drew raised an eyebrow. "You're in therapy?"

There was no reason to be surprised by his disbelief. Even she found it hard to believe. Instead of indulging him with the details about why she was seeing Dr. Raymond, she muttered, "I'm going to be late for work," and brushed past him toward the bedroom.

Rather than going to her closet, she sat on the edge of her unmade bed and covered her face with her hands. This was too much. Having her feelings about Drew flare up at the same time she was trying to convince herself some mad man wasn't going to use her for target practice was more than she could handle. Right now, she needed to focus on getting herself ready and going to work.

Mentally slamming the door on Drew's suggestion of reconciliation, she rose from the bed and went into the bathroom. She washed her face, brushed her teeth, applied makeup, and tried to do something with her mess of hair. The finished product was only slightly better than the beginning one. She looked like she'd been on an all-night bender and was trying to put herself back together. Contributing to that effect, she grabbed the outfit closest to her and threw it on.

I'm really going to turn heads today, she thought dryly.

Glancing at the bedside clock, she realized that if she left at that exact moment, she'd still be fifteen minutes late for work. She rushed from the bedroom and passed Drew, who was still standing in the kitchen.

"Lock up when you leave," she said as she opened the front door. With her hand still on the doorknob, she paused and turned back toward the kitchen. "Why was there blood on the wall next to the shower?"

Drew half smiled. "I cut myself shaving. You really need a new razor."

At that she walked out the door. On the way to the car, she heard Drew yell, "I'm just trying to help! You still need me, whether you want to admit it or not."

Tessa's life was off-kilter. She'd nearly unraveled because her ex-husband cut himself shaving. That sounded crazy, even for her. It sounded Mama crazy.

Not again, she scolded herself.

She was angry at Drew for his sudden intrusion into her life, but he was right. On that horrible night, she had called him, and she hated herself for it. Then she let him stay with her the last two nights.

Now he'd made it clear that he wanted to give their relationship another chance.

And she was the one who had to figure out what to do about it.

17

LOIS SIMMONS WIPED her hands on her apron and placed them on the edge of the kitchen counter, leaning closer to the window above it.

"I knew it!" she whispered to herself.

That same handsome man was stepping off the front stoop of the neighbor woman's house again.

He'd been there the past two nights, and she'd seen him leaving early in the morning wearing the same clothes he'd arrived in the night before.

"Good for her," Lois said to the empty kitchen. While she didn't believe women should be easy conquests, she was glad to see that Tessa might not be so lonely after all. "At least she has one person in her life," she continued.

Walter left for work an hour ago, and since then she'd been making conversation with an empty room. Walt always told her she didn't really need him to have a conversation, but he had no idea how right he was. All day long, she carried on conversations with thin air, but she'd never tell him there wasn't much of a difference between talking to him and talking to nobody at all. She couldn't bring herself to tell him, after thirty-five years of marriage, he was a bore to talk to. That would hurt his feelings.

While she was busily working to fill orders for her rapidly growing home-based bakery, Lois's Loaves, she had plenty of time to watch the neighborhood.

Without a commercial oven, she already had to scramble to get orders to her customers on time, and she certainly didn't have a moment to spare. On the other hand…

Curiosity getting the better of her, she again wiped her hands on her apron and patted her perfectly bobbed hair. Of course it looks okay, she reminded herself on the way out the kitchen door. You just had it done yesterday.

She rushed into her side yard just in time to hear the man answer his phone as he slid behind the steering wheel. As he backed out of the driveway, Lois put her hands on her ever-expanding hips.

Apparently, she wouldn't find out what was going on with him and her next-door neighbor after all. Not today, anyway.

18

DREW GROANED AS he glanced at his cell phone. He answered after the third ring, just before the call went to voice mail.

"Good morning, Camille," he said as he slid behind the steering wheel.

"Where have you been, Drew?" Camille demanded. "I stopped by your house this morning on my way to work, but you were already gone. Did you go to work early?"

He took a deep breath. He hated lying – was morally opposed to it, actually – but telling her the truth would start a conversation he didn't have the energy for. "I had to run out. I'm on my way back home now to get ready for work." That's not exactly a lie, he rationalized. I did run out. Last night.

"Well, I thought I'd surprise you with dinner last night, but you weren't home then, either. I called, but you didn't answer." Camille's voice was missing its usual playful tone. Drew suspected she knew something was up.

He pulled the phone away from his ear and checked the

call history. Sure enough, she'd called three times during the movie when he'd had his phone on silent.

"Is everything okay?" Camille's voice was softer now.

"Yes, of course," he assured her. "I've just got a lot on my mind these days."

"Okay." Camille paused. "So, where were you?"

Here we go, Drew thought. Whether he liked it or not, this conversation wouldn't wait. "I needed to meet somebody."

Silence floated between the two of them before she asked, "Is there someone else, Drew?"

He felt a stab of regret. Camille sounded hurt. "Not exactly…" That wasn't a lie, either. Tessa didn't seem to want him.

"Then where were you last night?" she asked for a third time.

"With an old friend." His vague answers were bound to confirm her suspicions.

"Who is she?" Camille demanded.

Drew got the impression Camille had been in this position before.

"Tessa."

"Tessa!" Camille shouted. "You mean your ex-wife, Tessa?"

"Yes."

"From the way you talked about her, she sounds like a nightmare."

Anger rose in Drew's chest. He and Tessa had definitely had their problems – this morning proved it. But hearing someone else call her a nightmare, made him feel both angry and ashamed. Why had he ever told Camille the reason they split up?

"She's not a nightmare, Camille," Drew said defensively.

"But what about her trust issues? You told me all about them. And what about her temper?"

"What about them?" he challenged. "She knows me and understands me more than anyone else ever has." He hesitated, then said quietly, "Or ever will."

The sharp intake of breath on the other end of the call told Drew that Camille understood what he meant. This relationship was a dead end, and now she knew it. He was relieved that it was finally out in the open.

"Did you spend the night with her?" Camille asked. Her voice was gentle, like a child's.

What a way to start the day, he thought. I've made two women mad at me in the span of thirty minutes, and I haven't even had breakfast.

"Yes, I stayed the night." He didn't elaborate. There was no need. Camille would feel betrayed no matter what.

She was crying softly in his ear as he pulled into the driveway of his house. He glanced at the clock on his dashboard. "We'll have to talk about this later. I've got a meeting and I'm running behind. How about we meet for lunch at the deli near your office?"

Through sniffles, Camille agreed.

Drew dreaded lunch but was looking forward to his relationship with Camille being over. He needed room to breathe, and he wanted to convince Tessa to make a go of it again.

As he rushed up the front steps of his house, he told himself that this time, no matter what happened, he wouldn't back out on Tessa.

19

CAMILLE WALKER DISCONNECTED the call with Drew, dropped her phone in her purse, and pulled a tissue from the box on her desk. She blew her nose and sniffed, a tear dropping from her cheek and wrinkling the new account paperwork on her desk. Dabbing her eyes, she shook her head.

This can't be happening, she thought. Drew is breaking up with me. I've finally found the kind of man I want to spend my life with, and he's on the verge of kicking me to the curb.

She tossed the used tissue into the trash can and grabbed a new one.

Here she was, in her early thirties, and for the first time in her life in a meaningful relationship. She'd relished the last three months. Drew, a man like none she'd ever met, treated her with respect. Ever since she was a teenager, she'd had a string of boyfriends who looked at her like she was a sports car they couldn't wait to drive.

But Drew was different. He opened doors for her and everything. For the first time in her whole life, a man wasn't just interested in taking her for a test drive.

Another tear plopped onto the paperwork.

Straightening her spine, she clenched her teeth and thrust her jaw forward. She wouldn't let him go without a fight. There had to be something more she could offer. Something Tessa couldn't.

Camille wasn't as successful as Drew, she knew, but she made a decent living, and she had one of the highest new account rates of any relationship banker at her branch. She'd been especially successful at getting men to open new or additional accounts they really didn't need. Her mouth curved into a slight smile. She'd used the tools at her disposal to make it almost impossible for clients to refuse, and those tools didn't have anything to do with low interest rates or high rates of return. No, Camille used the tools she'd been working with all her life: her looks and a low-cut neckline.

The way she wore them was almost an art. Few women appreciated it, but their husbands certainly did. Leaning close when talking, as if she were sharing a secret just between the two of them; looking up through expertly mascaraed lashes; leaving just the slightest hint of perfume in the air when she left a room. All those things worked like magic.

Except on Drew.

Oh sure, he appreciated her beauty. He'd have to be blind not to. She rarely had days when she felt unattractive, and that confidence was just another tool in her arsenal.

After blowing her nose one last time, she tossed the tissue in the trash can, slid her phone out of her purse, and punched the number for her best friend.

Beth would know what to do.

She knew what was coming at lunch, and no matter what it took, Camille wouldn't let Drew get away.

20

DETECTIVE AL JEFFERSON mopped his forehead with a handkerchief and tugged on the front of his suit, trying to get air flowing through his clothes. The hottest day of the year wasn't the time to be beating the pavement looking for a possible killer. The day was scorching, and he longed to be in his air-conditioned cruiser. Instead, he was following up on the lead Tessa James had given him the day before.

So far, he'd hit nothing but dead ends. Not that he was surprised. Even she'd doubted herself.

Most of the residents on the street were at work. *Of course they are,* he mused. *They have to pay for this lifestyle somehow.* A few housewives opened their doors, but he didn't get much from them.

He smirked again, thinking of them as housewives – he doubted any of them even lifted a finger around the house. The ones he'd actually gotten to talk to were either on their way to play tennis at "the club," about to go shopping, or out to lunch.

Of course, many of the women could have been executives, but they weren't home to be questioned.

Al fought off a pang of jealousy. For sitting around in an air-conditioned office all day, these people certainly were raking in the dough.

"Where's the justice in that?" he'd often complained to Darlene, his long-suffering girlfriend, when his choice of career had been put down by old schoolmates who went on to get multiple degrees and ended up working for Fortune 500 companies. "I get paid peanuts for putting my life on the line every day, and these guys sit around looking at paper all day and are worth millions."

Darlene would nod along, pretending she wasn't sick of hearing him complain, then end the conversation by telling him what a strong, handsome man he was, and that he didn't need to have a ton of money to make her happy.

It worked every time. When she got through with him, his insecurities were gone.

He stood on the sidewalk in front of the house at the end of the cul-de-sac, the one Tessa James had described. Even if she was wrong about what she saw, she was certainly right about one thing: the house definitely had a creepy vibe. He suddenly felt uneasy.

Walking up the front steps, he pressed the doorbell with his thumb. Chimes ding-donged inside. He waited for somebody to answer – not that he really expected them to.

Just as he gave up and began to descend the steps, the door swung open. In the doorway stood a man of average height with a slender build. His overall appearance was unremarkable. Except his eyes. There was something peculiar about them. If this was the guy, he knew what the James woman meant. As he looked at the man, her story gained credibility.

He extended his hand toward the man who opened the

door. "Hello, sir. I'm Detective Al Jefferson. I'd like to ask you a few questions about something that might have happened here two nights ago," he said as a bead of sweat rolled from his side burn and down his jaw line. "May I come in?"

"Actually," the man said, squeezing through the narrow doorway, "I was just going back to work. Do you mind if we walk and talk?" he asked, motioning toward a sleek silver sports car parked at the curb.

"Sure," Al agreed, eying the car.

"What can I do for you, Detective?" the man asked politely, turning to lock the front door.

The two men fell into step as they walked toward the car. "We had a report of a crime on this street Monday night. I'm questioning all the residents to see if they know anything about it."

"Crime? Here? I'm afraid not. Every home on this street has state-of-the-art security systems. A criminal wouldn't stand a chance here, I'm afraid," the man offered. He placed his hands on his hips and squinted into the sun.

"Well, sir," Detective Jefferson continued, "someone has come forward to say she witnessed a crime, and I have to check it out. You understand, I'm sure."

The man laughed a tight, high-pitched laughed. "Impossible. Nothing ever happens here. This is probably the safest street in the city, but I do understand that you have to poke around."

Al clenched his teeth. Poke around? "Okay. Thank you for your time. If you think of anything, please call," he said, extending a business card in the man's direction.

"Of course," the man mumbled as he pressed the button on his key fob to unlock his car. It beeped twice.

Al walked toward his own car, and behind him he heard the thump of the man's car door slamming shut. The engine roared to life, then the car sped past him, the driver never glancing at him as he drove by.

The detective opened his car door and slipped into the cruiser, turning the air-conditioning on full blast. As he pulled away from the curb, he made a mental note to take a closer look at the owner of that house.

21

FOR THE THIRD time in thirty-six hours, he gripped the steering wheel with sweaty hands, cursing himself for his carelessness. How had he let this happen? That woman had seen him, and in that moment of surprise he'd let his guard slip. They'd made eye contact and now he was being questioned by the police. Had anyone else seen him that night, too?

Did the detective believe him? He wasn't lying when he said this was probably the safest street in the city. It was – or at least it would be if he didn't live there.

It had been a stroke of luck that he was getting ready to go back to work after lunch when his doorbell rang. Theoretically, he should have been expecting a police officer to stop by, but he'd been genuinely surprised, and he was struck by momentary panic that the house hadn't been cleaned thoroughly.

That was ridiculous, of course. Nobody would find evidence there no matter how hard they tried.

Still, his carelessness made him doubt himself, and he didn't want that detective to have the chance to snoop around. As far as he was concerned, if there was any investigation at all, it was still in the beginning stages. His lips pulled back into a smile. It would be pretty hard for them to get any proof of a crime with no evidence and no victim.

Even so...

He slammed his palm against the steering wheel. "This is *not* the way it was supposed to go," he growled. "She would have never been missed if that nosy woman hadn't been on my street."

Then he'd been stupid enough to drive all over the place last night looking for her.

What if she'd seen him? She'd go to the cops again before he had a chance to take care of her.

As he pulled into the parking lot at his office, he vowed that she wouldn't get the chance and assured himself that she wouldn't be a threat much longer. This time, though, he was going to make sure he did it right.

22

TESSA'S PALMS GREW sweaty as she held the phone to her ear. "What do you mean, you haven't found anything? I saw it."

"I know what you saw, Ms. James, but we haven't found a body matching the description you gave us. It's been more than twenty-four hours since you came to us, and so far, we haven't found a single thing suggesting there was a crime."

"That doesn't mean nothing happened," Tessa countered. "There are a lot of places a person could stash a body."

"That's true. I'm looking into this, and I've questioned the people who live on that street, including the owner of that house. Most of them were incredulous that anyone would even suggest anything bad could happen in their own little corner of paradise."

"That only means those people can't face the idea that they're not as safe as they think they are," Tessa said, her face hot.

In a soothing tone, Detective Jefferson said, "I'm not saying I don't believe you; I'm saying that I haven't come up with anything to support your claim."

Tessa heard the detective take a deep breath on the other end of the line before he continued. "There have been no new missing persons reported in the last day and a half. So, as you can see, my hands are tied. Until we find a body or get a report that a woman matching the description you gave us is missing, there's nothing else I can do. I'm sorry."

Activity buzzed around her. Business as usual in the newsroom. A cameraman and a reporter were heading out the side door to a news van, on their way to a breaking story. Tessa squelched the hope that the body of a young woman had been found. From the way her conversation with Detective Jefferson was going, she doubted whether anyone was even seriously looking.

"Of course, I would be grateful for any more information you have," he added in what Tessa assumed was a feeble attempt to appease her, "but at the moment we have nothing to go on."

"I see," Tessa whispered, feeling small and insignificant. The detective's meaning was clear: until they had some kind of evidence, they weren't going to keep looking.

Feeling completely helpless, she pushed away the image of a field mouse scampering through the grass, desperately trying to get away from the bird of prey waiting to swoop down and grab her. The room spun. Tessa grabbed the edge of her desk to steady herself, angry at herself for being so scared and angry at Detective Jefferson for not doing more to protect her.

I'm not crazy! she wanted to scream. *I know I saw it!* Maybe if she said it loud enough, she'd be able to convince herself. She bit her lip to stop herself.

Until something turned up, though, she'd feel like a nut for going to the police with something she wasn't even sure of.

"Of course, we'll let you know if there are any developments," the detective said. "I'm sure you understand."

"Yes. I understand. But Detective, hear me clearly: I don't intend to become his next victim. Find that body," she demanded, her anger strengthening her voice.

His voice softened. "Trust me when I tell you we'll do everything we can to keep that from happening, Ms. James."

She pushed the disconnect button on her cell phone and laid it on her desk, suddenly thankful for the claustrophobia-inducing cubicle. At least the makeshift walls gave her some measure of privacy.

Still dizzy, Tessa grabbed her purse and walked quickly past her coworkers and out into the sunshine. She needed air. The lunch rush foot traffic enclosed her from all sides. She gulped the summer heat, mouth dry and throat parched. Breaking free from the crowd, she walked to Chester's Deli, one of her favorite places, for iced tea. Tessa stopped just outside the door.

Seated at a small table in front of the window were Drew and a woman with honey-colored hair. Sliding her arm across the gray and white checkered tablecloth, the woman kept reaching for his hand. Her eyes were rimmed with tears. Tessa felt the familiar stab of pain when she saw Drew, then realized with a sinking stomach that he was probably in a relationship with this woman.

How could she not have suspected there would be someone else? He was smart, handsome, and successful.

The idea that he'd moved on from her stung. They were divorced and he was free to move on. She just hadn't expected to be replaced so quickly. If he was in a relationship, what was all his talk about them getting back together about?

Seeing him with another woman reminded her how

far-reaching the consequences of her distrust were. It was the reason he'd left her in the first place.

She found herself wondering if she distrusted humanity so much that her mind had fabricated a terrible event just because that was what she expected people to do to each other.

Something has to change, she told herself. I can't go on living like this and expecting the worst from people.

As she used her shoulders to shield herself from the crush of people around her, she pulled her cell phone from her purse and dialed the number she feared would become as familiar as her own.

Biting her lip, she spoke to the person who answered her call. "I need help."

23

"THIS MUST BE serious if you can't wait until next week for our regular session," Dr. Raymond said as he eased himself into his wingback chair.

"It is." Tessa glanced out the window behind Dr. Raymond. The sun was shining, and puffy clouds sailed effortlessly across the sky. If only life could be like that, she thought ruefully. How can I tell a mental health professional that I'm starting to wonder if I really am going crazy?

Like Mama.

Dr. Raymond scratched his jaw line where the shadow of a beard was starting to fill in. "Go on," he said.

"Well," she began. "It's just that I..." Tessa clenched her jaw and willed herself to continue. "A couple days ago – Monday to be exact – I thought I saw something. But now I'm not so sure."

Nodding his head, Dr. Raymond said, "I see," in the way that only shrinks can. "Tell me what you saw."

After telling the story to Dr. Raymond, Tessa sank back into the chair and waited.

He nodded in response, more to himself than to her. He was still scratching his growing beard. "You're right," he said finally. "That is serious."

"Did I really see it?" Tessa asked. "The detective I spoke to said there was no evidence that anything actually happened, and they haven't found a body. No missing persons reports have been filed. As far as he's concerned, there's nothing to investigate." Tessa plucked the cuff of her shirt. "Did I just pull this whole situation out of thin air?"

"Do *you* think you pulled it out of thin air?"

Tessa shrugged. "It wouldn't be the first time…"

Dr. Raymond leaned forward. "Tell me about that."

Taking a deep breath, she said, "When Mama died, I thought I saw someone – a man – running through the back-yard. By the time the police and the paramedics got there, he was long gone. They checked for footprints, fingerprints, everything, but couldn't come up with anything. They said it's common for people who have experienced emotional trauma to be confused about what exactly happened. That it's the mind's way of protecting itself."

"For some people, that's true," Dr. Raymond offered, "but not for everybody." He scanned his notes. "So, two nights ago, through the window of a house in The Estates, you saw the body of a young woman wrapped in plastic sheeting, being carried over someone's shoulder?"

"Yes," Tessa said firmly.

"I noticed you started fidgeting with your shirt cuff when you were telling me about the detective. What worries you most about that?" he asked softly.

"Right now, I just feel like I'm walking around with a target on my back, and the police can't do anything to stop it."

"It sounds like you believe it really happened," Dr. Raymond observed aloud.

"I do. I know they haven't found a body, but that doesn't mean he didn't just find a clever place to hide it, right? I mean, when they have a reason to start looking, I really think they'll find something."

Dr. Raymond leaned back in his chair and crossed his ankle over his knee, revealing argyle socks in shades of blue. He made a few notes, then replied, "What's important is that you're absolutely positive about what you saw. Are you?"

"Yes!" Tessa said emphatically. "I saw a man carrying a woman wrapped in plastic over his shoulder. And what really scares me is that I'm pretty sure he saw me, too. He looked straight in my direction. Right now, it feels like everything my mother ever taught me is true."

Dr. Raymond made a note then looked at her again. "Clearly you don't feel safe, and from the impression I've gotten, you never really have. Is that a fair assessment?"

Tessa thought a moment. "Yes, that's true."

"What we want to do is figure out what it will take for you to feel safe, like you can let your guard down and not be on defense all the time. What will it take for you to feel like somebody isn't just waiting to pounce on you when you're not looking?" Dr. Raymond's pen was poised and ready to go.

She turned her head and watched a bird that was perched on the windowsill. It was completely alone, but it seemed content, and she knew any sudden movement would startle it, and it would fly to safety.

"I've convinced myself I'm tough and independent, and for the most part I am. But when this… fear gets set off, just having somebody with me who I *could* trust would help." Her thoughts wandered to Drew. "Unfortunately, the only person who has ever come close is currently unavailable."

"I see. And who is that?"

"My ex-husband, Drew, but he's involved with someone. I doubt either of them want me running to him in my time of need." Again, Tessa glanced at the bird. "They might just want me to disappear. He is the one who ended things between us, after all. My inability to trust him just got to be too much."

"Are you certain he wouldn't be willing to help?" Dr. Raymond challenged.

Tessa sighed. Drew had proved in the last couple days that he was but seeing him with that woman at lunch today also proved he wasn't waiting around for her to learn how to trust him. "I don't know," she said honestly.

When her fifty minutes was up, she stood, startling the bird that just moments before had been contentedly soaking up the sunshine. As it flew away, Tessa wondered if she would ever stop living like that scared little bird.

24

SCRATCHING HIS GROWING beard, Dr. Raymond made a mental note to shave it off as soon as he got home. Fran, his late wife, always said he'd look ridiculous with a beard.

He caught his reflection in the fish tank. Of course, Fran had been right. With his thinning hair and bushy eyebrows, the beard made his face look too heavy. Add to that the bizarre black and silver streaks that made him look like a zebra, and his reflection was every bit as ridiculous as Fran had warned. And he couldn't stop scratching. It probably looked like he had fleas.

Watching the fish swim back and forth in the tank, Dr. Raymond wondered what to do about Tessa James. He'd recently started cutting back on his practice, but he'd decided one more new client would be okay. If he'd denied her or tried to refer her to another psychologist, he had the hunch she would never get the help she needed. Now that he'd met her, he saw how difficult it must have been for her to make that phone call. The fact that she'd asked him to squeeze her in today delighted him. She saw the need to open up to another person and came back only two days later when she needed someone to talk to. It saddened him, though, because he knew she probably didn't have anyone else.

She'd grown up with a sick and paranoid mother who taught Tessa to distrust not only other people, but she'd also poisoned her mind so much that she didn't even trust herself.

The most challenging clients he'd ever had were the ones like Tessa's mother. They didn't want help. Typically, they'd stay in therapy only a few weeks, or as long as their families could convince them to come. During those few sessions, the clients would either shut him out completely or hurl insults at him for digging into their personal business.

The children of those parents didn't fare much better, usually because they'd been so conditioned to keep everyone at arm's length that they struggled to have meaningful interpersonal relationships.

Tessa was walking proof of that. Her self-imposed isolation was heartbreaking, and though she expended vast amounts of energy to appear strong, her composure had nearly crumbled when he asked about friends and family. She was alone, and it was her own doing.

He flipped through the notes he'd taken Monday, at Tessa's initial session. As a child, she'd taken sole responsibility of playing watchdog after her father left. She'd stayed up all night so her mother could sleep. Dr. Raymond knew very well how damaging that kind of sleep deprivation could be to a child's growing brain, not to mention the weight of caring for a mentally ill parent. In fact, he was surprised that Tessa functioned as well as she did, considering her upbringing.

She needed help now, before the distrust planted by her mother ruined her.

25

TESSA PULLED HER six-year-old Toyota into the driveway. Even though she'd just picked it up from the mechanic, it still sputtered.

Her heart sank when she saw Drew sitting on her front stoop, chin resting in his hands. She thought about putting the car in reverse and getting out of there without talking to him, but that wouldn't solve anything.

She parked but waited until Drew stood and walked toward her before getting out of the car. Those few moments to compose herself would have to do. After all these years, Drew still commanded her attention. He'd always had that effect on women.

Obviously.

He opened the car door for her, and she dreaded the conversation about to happen. "Sorry, baby. A man's got needs, ya know?"

Tessa immediately dismissed the idea. He had friends who would say something like that, but Drew wouldn't. He was a class act and had been nothing but faithful through their entire fourteen-year relationship.

She got out of the car and allowed him to close the door behind her. "I went to your office to see you, but Jack said you'd left for the day. I think he's worried about you."

"I had an appointment," Tessa said, leaving it at that.

"I see." Drew's eyes scanned the street. "Listen, Tess, we need to talk. About what you saw at lunch – "

Tessa held up a hand to stop him. "Drew, it's fine. Really. It stung, I'll admit that, but we haven't been together for a year. I don't have a claim on you, and I shouldn't have been surprised to see you with someone."

Drew watched the children across the street squeal as they ran through the sprinkler in their yard. "Well, I was breaking up with her, for what it's worth. A buddy of mine set us up on a blind date a few months ago. We had a good time, but she was taking it a little more seriously than I was."

Tessa shifted her weight, adjusted her shoulder bag, and squinted into the sun. "She's very beautiful," she said, suddenly aware of the five pounds she could never seem to lose.

"She is," Drew agreed. "But that's as far as it goes. She's not my type, and she always tried to keep tabs on me. She never wanted to let me out of her sight. It kind of made me miss the days of you keeping me at arm's length. At least you were a challenge." He grinned.

Tessa smiled. It was the first time her neurotic need to keep people at a distance had been described as anything but maddening. "I'm sorry she wasn't right for you," she said, again looking off into the distance.

"No, you're not," Drew said, taking a step closer to her. "And neither am I."

As they stood, each with their gaze purposefully fixed on something other than one another the sound of a car engine broke into Tessa's thoughts. As she tore her eyes from the flowers lining her front walk, the image of a dark blue sedan forced its way into her awareness. As it passed, Tessa strained to see the driver through the heavily tinted windows.

As Tessa turned her back to the road so the driver couldn't see her face, a loud pop exploded from the car and Tessa dropped to the ground.

26

AS TESSA LAY on the ground, arms covering her head, Drew squatted next to her.

"Are you okay?" he asked, alarm filling his voice.

"Yes." Her voice was muffled as she spoke into her arms.

Drew grabbed her elbow and gave it a gentle tug, encouraging Tessa to get to her feet. "Are you sure?"

Tessa nodded. She brushed the grass clippings from her pants and stood with her shoulders back. The children across the street had stopped running through the sprinkler and were staring in her direction. She forced a smile and waved, then turned and went inside.

"What was that?" Drew asked once the door was shut behind them.

"I think a car backfired."

"I know that," he said. "I meant your reaction. It was a bit of an overreaction, don't you think?"

Tessa didn't answer.

Using his thumb and index finger, he lifted her chin so her eyes would meet his. "Are you that scared?"

Tears stung the backs of Tessa's eyes. She blinked them away and pulled her chin from his grasp. "Stop. You're going to make me rust."

"I know you're strong, Tess, but even you need help sometimes." Drew's mouth was a hard, straight line. "Will you please let me help you?"

Tessa sighed. "You have been helping me, Drew, but I can't depend on that forever. Seeing you with your girlfriend today reminded me of that. Somehow during the past couple days I'd forgotten."

"You *can* depend on me. I'll keep you safe," Drew promised.

Tessa shook her head. "You can't. Not forever. I appreciate everything you've done, I really do, but I have to remember how to stand on my own." She took a deep breath and forced her chest forward. She could take care of herself. She'd done it for years.

Drew slapped his leg. "I don't get you Tessa. First, you're mad at me for bringing you dinner, then you call me when you need help. I come, and you let me stay here with you for two nights. Now it sounds like you're kicking me out the door."

Tessa winced. He didn't understand. Neither did she, for that matter. All she knew was that seeing him with that woman had reminded her she was on her own. "I can't keep going on like this, Drew," she said quietly. "I can't get used to having you around again. When we go back to our own lives, I don't want to have to start over again. It was hard enough the first time."

"Who says we have to go back to our own lives?" Drew asked, his eyes searching Tessa's face.

"You did," she said simply. "When you left."

His head jerked back as though she'd slapped him. "So that's it then. No second chances?"

"I can take care of myself," Tessa said evenly.

Drew narrowed his eyes and studied her. "You almost sound like you believe that. But what about the guy who might be looking for you? You couldn't fake that reaction to the car backfiring. You're terrified."

"I can take care of myself," she repeated. "It's not your job to take care of me. It seems I've forgotten that."

Drew's face turned red. "You're impossible, you know that?" he said. Then turned and walked out the front door.

27

TESSA SQUINTED INTO the setting sun as she watched Drew drive away. After Mama died, sunset became one of Tessa's favorite things, but not for the reason most people loved it. Sure, it was beautiful, but for Tessa, sunset represented freedom. Freedom from being her mom's protector. That was one of the life lessons she'd learned from her mother. Tessa remembered watching Mama dance around at sunset because her monsters hadn't gotten her that day, even though they both new her monsters roared loudest at night. Then she'd dance again at sunrise because she'd survived the night.

Tessa knew very well that the darkest hours were just after sunset and right before sunrise.

But she could take care of herself. She had to.

As a child, she'd check every closet and look under every bed, assuring Mama there was nothing lurking in the darkness. She'd never known if what she was looking for was real or imagined, but somehow it didn't matter. Sometimes her assurance was enough to calm Mama down. Sometimes no power on earth could do it.

For the past few nights, sunset hadn't represented freedom. She'd survived the day, yes, but once darkness settled in, Tessa worried about a whole different kind of monster: a killer on the loose that she could only pray didn't have her face burned into his mind.

When Drew was there, she could relax a little. Someone else was on the lookout for the monster, the way she used to do for Mama.

Dr. Raymond was right. Tessa needed to feel safe, and Drew was the closest she'd ever come. But she'd asked him to leave, pushing the only safety net she'd ever had out her front door.

She only vaguely remembered her father being around. The crazy had been too much for him, and, when Tessa was six, he took off. Given the choice, she might have done the same thing. If she were honest with herself, she'd never really forgiven him for leaving her with such a sick and unstable mother. She understood him but had never been able to forgive him.

Ironically, the more Tessa came to understand why he left, the stronger her urge to stay close to Mama. She'd needed to be protected.

Protected from what? Tessa asked herself countless times through the long years she'd played watchdog. At first, it was only from the bad people Mama said were out to get her. She'd stay up half the night watching for them, many times falling asleep on the stairs.

Even then, Tessa thought, it was unreasonable to put that kind of pressure on myself. But Mama was so weak, so frail, that she needed somebody to take care of her. The sicker she got, though, the more Tessa realized that what Mama really needed protection from was herself.

Seeing her gently swaying from the second-floor banister had confirmed that.

Tessa turned from the window. The sun had dipped behind the trees, leaving behind only an orange glow.

Darkness would be here soon.

Hungry but emotionally drained, Tessa grabbed a frozen dinner and popped it into the microwave. She couldn't even remember the last time she'd cooked a decent meal. With nobody there to share it with, it hardly seemed worth the effort.

The microwave beeped to tell her another culinary masterpiece was ready. Sometimes Tessa bothered to take it out of the plastic container and put it on a real plate, but tonight wasn't one of those times. She grabbed a potholder and slid it underneath the half-melted tray and snagged a fork from the drawer on her way out of the kitchen.

After settling onto the sofa, she grabbed the remote and flipped on the TV. She picked up her dinner, kicked her feet up on the coffee table, and blew on the steam billowing from the limp pasta.

Losing herself in someone else's life sounded like heaven, but the only thing on TV were crime dramas. She had no interest in crime at the moment, and her life was filled with enough of her own drama. She didn't need fictional drama, too.

Taking the last bite of pasta, she clicked the TV off and picked up a book she'd started last week. She only made it one chapter before the main character realized someone was lurking around outside her secluded home. At that moment, Tessa could have sworn she heard footsteps outside.

She tossed the book aside and dropped to the floor. Maybe she was overreacting, but Mama had always taught her to be afraid of things that go bump in the night.

From around the coffee table, she peered out the window as much as she could without getting off the floor. There was nothing there. Tessa gave herself a mental slap for being such a sissy and stood, trying to recover her dignity. The fact that no one saw her didn't make it any less embarrassing.

Twice in one evening she'd dropped to the ground because of the noise on her street. First a car, and now footsteps. Normal sounds were suddenly making her jump out of her skin.

Tessa took the plastic container from the frozen dinner to the kitchen trash. As she walked back through the living room toward the bedroom, she snapped off the lamp beside the sofa. As she passed the same window she'd looked out just moments before, she instinctively checked it one more time. Old habits and all.

There, staring back at her was the face of someone she didn't know, but someone who looked familiar, and whose eyes she wouldn't soon forget.

28

HEART THUDDING IN her chest, Tessa opened her front door and crept around to the side of the house. Her fight-or-flight instinct, which usually could go either way, had surprised her by sending her outside toward the prowler.

I must be out of my mind. The thought was nearly drowned out by the sound of her own beating heart.

As she turned the corner, back pressed against the brick, her survival instinct, now in overdrive, urged her to defend herself.

There, standing in front of the shrubs, was the honey-haired beauty she'd seen with Drew at lunch. She was wearing a jogging suit, and her hair was in a ponytail, bangs and fly-aways contained with a stretchy headband. Tonight, she looked much less like the vixen who'd been dining with Tessa's ex-husband and more like the girl next door. Under the streetlights, her eyes looked shadowed and puffy.

Drew said they broke up, Tessa thought. She'd been there. Losing Drew had hurt. It still did.

Camille stood there in the dark, eyes searching Tessa's face. She didn't say anything.

Tessa broke the silence. "Care to explain why you were looking through the window of my house?" The anxiety of seeing a stranger peeking through her window had settled, and her voice was calm.

"I needed to see you with my own eyes," Camille said softly.

"Why?" Even though this woman was clearly upset, and Tessa could empathize with her, a person would have to be pretty unhinged to stare through someone else's window at night.

"I needed to see you," Camille said, her eyes scanning the length of Tessa's body.

"How did you know where I live?"

"I followed Drew here. At a safe distance of course," Camille confessed. She crossed her arms over her full chest. "Drew dumped me today. He said I would never understand him the way you do. He still loves you." Camille's voice cracked. "I wanted to see why."

For possibly the first time in her life, Tessa was speechless. What exactly had Drew said to Camille?

Then she remembered Drew's words. He'd told her that he missed her and wanted to give it another try. But why would he want her, with all her baggage, over Camille the beauty queen?

If he did, score one for the home team. It was a victory for regular girls everywhere.

Then she remembered how angry Drew was when he left this evening. It seemed like any shot of reconciliation was gone. Besides, she wasn't even sure if she'd want to get back together.

"Look," Tessa said, "I'm not competition. Drew and I are divorced. That's the extent of our relationship."

"But he spent the night with you twice this week," Camille whined.

Tessa clamped her lips together, forcing herself not to laugh. This chick was crazy, and Tessa knew crazy. That was something they had in common. She made a mental note to ask Drew why all the women he fell for had a few screws loose.

"Yes, he spent the night here. But he slept on the couch. Alone."

Camille perked up. "Really?"

"Yes, really. Now, if you don't mind, I'm going back inside, and you need to get off my property." Tessa turned and started walking back around the house toward the front door. She stopped and turned to face Camille. "Don't ever come back here and press your nose against my window. Understand?" she warned.

Camille nodded. "Sorry for scaring you."

Tessa ignored her, walked into the house, and slammed the front door. As she engaged the deadbolt, Tessa thought, At least this time it was just a lovesick woman.

Next time, I might not be so lucky.

29

THURSDAY MORNING, TESSA could hardly wait to get to work. After what could only be described as a near home invasion by Camille last night, she felt even less safe in her house than she had before.

What if the face I'd seen hadn't been Camille's?

A piece of breakable glass was all that stood between her and a would-be killer. That knowledge made her realize just how vulnerable she was.

Tessa threw back the covers and grabbed her robe. After getting only a few hours of sleep, she needed coffee. While it was perking, she took a quick shower then preheated the oven. She grabbed a couple frozen biscuits and dropped them with a clang on the baking sheet. As they were baking, she booted up her laptop to check her email. As expected, there were dozens of emails about deals retailers thought she just couldn't pass up.

As if on autopilot, she clicked on the boxes to the left of each junk message. Just as she was about to hit delete, the subject line of the last one made her stop cold.

You're Next.

Taking a deep breath, Tessa moved the cursor to the subject line and clicked. The coffee pot gurgled in the background. The smell that usually revitalized her now made her nauseous.

She read the short message over and over.

Forget what you saw. Don't tell anybody. I'm watching.

That was it. The message was simple but clear.

How did he get my email address? Tessa thought frantically. He knows who I am. He found me. Her pulse quickened.

The image of the dead woman surged into the forefront of her mind. The email was more than a warning. Tessa already knew what this monster was capable of, and she'd already told people about it. Drew, Detective Jefferson, and Dr. Raymond all knew what she'd seen. Would they be in danger, too?

Detective Jefferson said he'd talked to the man who lived in that house, so he already knew she'd gone to the police. But surely the detective wouldn't have given him her information.

Logically, she knew he wouldn't have done that, but paranoia had set in. Mama's voice, from somewhere deep in her mind, told her that of course he would have. That's what people do.

Fear squeezed her throat.

The car backfire could have easily been a gunshot. The face pressed against her living room window could have very well been her would-be murderer instead of a slightly unhinged woman wanting her boyfriend back.

You're Next.

She would be. Tessa was certain of that.

30

HE TAPPED HIS pen nervously on his desk. Only eight thirty. The workday had just begun and all he wanted to do was leave. He loved his job, but the for the past few days he'd felt the net closing in on him.

That woman had seen him. He'd known that even before that detective came poking around.

It had been a stroke of luck that she was out in her front yard when he drove by. All he'd needed to do was find out the name of the woman that lived in that house.

Tessa James.

From there, just one call to a cousin who worked for an internet security company who fancied himself an overpaid hacker, and he had her email address. He hoped the message he'd sent would push her into hiding and she'd be too scared to leave her house. It's so much easier to hit a target when it's not moving.

The one thing he cursed himself about was that blasted rental car. After noticing how much his own vehicle would stick out in her neighborhood, he'd rented one that would blend in. Unfortunately, it had backfired just as he drove by her house.

He smirked as he remembered the loud *pop!* and the way she dropped to the ground and covered her head. She was scared, all right, and the email would certainly push her even farther down that path.

As he was relishing the way he'd gotten into that woman's head, his cell phone rang. His wife.

"I hate to tell you this, but I've got a crisis in Omaha, and I'm going to have to fly directly there. It looks like I won't be home for a few more days," she said in a regretful tone.

He smiled. "That's too bad. Do what you need to do."

After a quick goodbye, he slid the phone back into his briefcase. Leaning back in his chair, he relished his good luck. Things were working out. He had at least two more days to figure out what to do with the body.

That also gave him time to dispose of his other complication...

31

TESSA PRINTED THE email and stuffed it in her purse, then tossed the burned biscuits in the trash.

Maybe now she had the evidence the police needed. Maybe that detective would finally start acting like a crime happened, and not a moment too soon. She was beginning to wonder how long her sanity would hold out.

After calling Jack to let him know she'd be late for work again, she drove to the police station, hoping Detective Jefferson would be in.

The same desk sergeant greeted her, then then told her to wait in the same cold plastic chair. When she was finally escorted to Detective Jefferson's desk, she couldn't help but notice the difference in the man's appearance.

The detective's broad shoulders were slumped, his hair tousled, and dark circles rested under each eye. Tessa felt a moment of compassion and a fleeting feeling of guilt. She was bringing him something that would further complicate his day, but the guilt was gone as quickly as it had come. There was a killer out there, and now he was threatening her.

Detective Jefferson looked up as she sat down, then watched her hand dig into her shoulder bag and withdraw a piece of paper.

"I got this email this morning," Tessa said as she slid the paper across the desk.

He picked it up and read it. She watched his eyes track the words several times before he laid it on his desk. He rubbed the stubble on his face, then ran his fingers through his already unkempt hair. "This is very serious."

"I agree. Is it enough to start treating what I saw like an actual case?"

The detective sighed heavily. "Yes. You're being threatened and we don't take that lightly." He motioned toward the print-out. "This guy admitted to a crime, and this email more than suggests that you're also in danger."

Tessa shuddered.

"I am going to have a patrol car drive by your house every hour, to keep an eye on the place. Unfortunately, I can't offer more at the moment. We can work to get you into a safe house if you're willing to go, but that could take a little time," he offered.

Fear and Tessa's own stubbornness vied for her primary emotion about the safe house. On one hand, clearly this monster knew enough about her to have gotten his hands on her email address, and the idea of having someone watching for him, and being there to keep him from getting to her, could bring her a rare feeling of safety. On the other hand, taking care of Mama had fostered a fierce independent streak in her, and she certainly didn't want to leave her home, or depend on someone else to protect her.

"That's fine," Tessa said. "Can I have some time to think about it?"

"Of course." Detective Jefferson picked up the email. "I need to hang on to this for the file. Also, I'll need the tech guys to look at your computer to see if we can trace an IP address."

Tessa nodded. "Of course." She stood. "I'll let you know what I decide about the safe house."

She turned and walked out of the police station. This was all too much. But at least something was happening, and maybe they'd nail this guy before he had a chance to follow through on his threat.

32

DREW TRIED TO focus on the new client paperwork he was holding. Last night's argument with Tessa was occupying way more space in his mind than the asset transfer paperwork of his newest client.

Shoving away the memory of walking out on Tessa again after he vowed he would do whatever he could to help her, he zeroed in on the type of advising the new client would need.

He was a psychiatrist with more money than he'd ever spend, considering the bank statements that showed, aside from his house and the luxury car his wife had purchased, he lived like a miser.

Now that's a weird guy, Drew thought, wondering how a psychiatrist hadn't picked up on basic social cues. It seemed like he either made too much eye contact or not enough. When he spoke about his job, though, he did seem to thoroughly enjoy his work.

Is Tessa seeing someone like him? he wondered. Her admission about seeing a shrink had blindsided him, but it had also given him hope that she was beginning to see her need to change.

In a way, Drew was jealous. Tessa was opening up to a stranger in a way she hadn't with him during their ten-year marriage.

He picked up his cell phone, then laid it back on his desk. He'd almost called Tessa a dozen times. He owed her an apology and he wanted to make sure she'd been okay during the night.

Finding out he was involved with someone else had visibly hurt her.

Maybe she cares more than I realized, Drew thought, staring absently at the computer screen.

Tessa was unlike any woman he'd ever met, and not only because half the time she was nearly impossible to live with. She had a brain and wasn't afraid to use it. She was always thrilled to have a good debate and never failed to call him on his bull. She had a brain and a backbone, a combination that would be threatening to a lot of guys he knew.

Glancing at the clock in the corner of his computer screen, he saw that it was a half hour before he usually took his lunch break. He grabbed his keys from his desk drawer and walked past his assistant, Dorothy and out into the thick summer air.

He went to Chester's Deli, where he'd broken up with Camille only yesterday, and ordered Tessa's favorite – a ham and swiss on a Kaiser roll with extra mustard – then waited in a seat by the counter. When his number was called, he grabbed the bag and darted out the door. Tessa never went out for lunch, and he wanted to catch her before she heated up one of those awful microwaveable meals she practically lived on.

He unlocked the driver's side door, slid behind the steering wheel, and set the bag on the passenger seat. As he pulled out of his parking space, he couldn't shake the feeling that someone was watching him.

33

CAMILLE SNIFFED AND wiped her eyes with the balled-up tissue clutched in her right hand. Ever since she found out Drew was interested in someone else – his ex-wife, no less – she'd been questioning everything about herself. How could he not think they were right for each other?

She knew she'd never be the smartest girl in the room, but until now she'd never needed to be. Drew always wanted to talk about what was going on in the world, what the economy would look like over the next several months, and debate politics. Though she didn't understand most of it, she thought she'd done a pretty good job faking it.

"Maybe I'll never be good enough!" Camille whined to her best friend, Beth. "Why is it that when a good guy finally comes along, he doesn't want me?" Camille blew her nose again.

"I don't know," Beth soothed. "I'm sorry I ever told Pete you would be a good match for Drew. I just thought after everything I'd heard about his ex-wife, you might be a nice change for him."

Camille huffed and plunked the box of tissues on the coffee table.

"If it makes you feel any better, I think you would have ended up being miserable in the long run," Beth offered.

"It doesn't make me feel better. Nothing will make me feel better ever again. If you could have seen him, Beth. He went back to Chester's today. I was sitting right there, and he never even looked at me. When his order was ready, he snatched it up and practically ran to his car." A tear dropped onto the front of her shirt. "Or maybe he did notice me and was just trying to avoid me. She drained the last bit of wine in her glass and held it out to Beth. "I need more."

Beth unfolded her long legs and stood, then took the glass from Camille's hand. "He's not worth your tears, honey," Beth assured as she walked toward the kitchen.

"But how do I convince him I'm the one he wants?" Camille asked, picking an imaginary piece of lint off her pants.

"You're absolutely positive he wants to get back together with his ex-wife?" Beth asked, filling the glass to the rim.

Camille nodded. "That's sure what it sounded like to me. He told me I'd never understand him the way she does. He even spent the night with her!" she wailed and plucked another tissue from the box.

Beth deposited the wine glass on the table in front of her friend and folded herself back up in the club chair. "Maybe he just needs to be reminded of all the things she did that drove him nuts," she suggested.

"I tried that. He just got mad. He knows what's wrong with her and he still loves her." Camille lifted the wine glass and guzzled. She lowered it to the coffee table with a clank and pointed to it. "More."

Beth shot her friend a disapproving look. "You're going to get yourself drunk."

"Good," Camille said as she closed her eyes and rested her head on the back of the sofa. "I just want to forget this ever happened."

When Beth returned from the kitchen, she put the glass directly in Camille's hand, set the bottle down in front of her, and plopped back in the chair. "Don't asked me to get up again," she gently warned.

Camille took a long drink and said, "You know something? She seems perfectly nice. When I went to her house last night and pressed my face against the window, she didn't call the cops or try to shoot me or anything. She just came outside and talked to me. I think she was mad that I was there, but I think I get why Drew loves her," Camille slurred.

At that, the empty wineglass slipped from Camille's hand and her head fell backward. Soon she was snoring.

34

TESSA'S HEART BEAT faster as she drove down Oak Street, probably named for the giant tree at the end of the cul-de-sac. Images from Monday night bombarded her mind, the clarity of them making her shiver.

Am I crazy for making this trip? Tessa asked herself for the thirtieth time in as many minutes. Detective Jefferson offered a safe house, and instead I'm parked near the most *un*safe house I can think of.

But she had to know. If she was going to go into hiding, she needed to make sure her imagination wasn't getting the better of her.

She unbuckled her seatbelt and got out of the car. The thump of the car door shutting echoed on the otherwise silent street. Tessa wrapped her arms around her waist, fighting every urge to hop back in the car and leave.

Placing one hand on the roof to steady herself, she glanced around the neighborhood. In the daylight, it was even more impressive. Gorgeous houses, luxury cars, immaculate landscaping. Despite having seen the woman's dead body thrown over that man's shoulder, Tessa wondered how something like that could happen on a street like this.

This was the American Dream – or something like that – and as far as Tessa knew, the American Dream didn't include murder.

At least, not for most people.

The house in question sat peacefully at the end of the court. Today, in the sunshine, it didn't look quite as haunted.

Tessa walked to the spot on the sidewalk where she had been standing Monday night. She squinted to get a better look into the front room of the house. It looked ordinary. Glancing at the hedges she'd hidden behind while her mind tried to process what she'd seen, she thought about last night, when Camille was looking through her window.

The people who live here would have thought I was either a burglar or a crazy person and would have called the police, Tessa thought. On the heels of that thought came another one: if they had called the police, maybe she wouldn't be in this mess.

Satisfied that the police would eventually arrest the murderer, she got back in the car and turned around at the end of the cul-de-sac, slowing as she drove back past the house in question. It seemed perfectly lovely, like nothing bad could ever happen there.

Unfortunately, Tessa knew better.

35

STILL DISAPPOINTED FROM having missed Tessa at her office, Drew returned to work.

"Is everything okay, Mr. James?" Dorothy asked.

"Yes. Thank you, Dorothy," he replied as he walked into his office and closed the door. How many times did he have to tell her to stop calling him Mr. James? He was thirty-six; Dorothy was fifty-two.

Knowing he shouldn't be this upset about missing the chance to surprise Tessa, he glanced over his to-do list for the afternoon. Of course, it wasn't missing Tessa that upset him, it was the way he'd left things with her last night. Pushing the thought away, he looked at the item at the top of his list. A particularly high-strung client who was always worried about her money wanted him to call her. More than once he'd told her she'd be better off moving her money somewhere else if she couldn't trust him to handle it. So far, she hadn't, and he was stuck dealing with her insecurities.

As he was trying to muster up the will to call her, his cell phone rang. He checked the caller ID and answered.

"Thanks for lunch," Tessa said. "You've been feeding me well this week."

He smiled. Her voice was certainly warmer than it had been last night. "You're welcome. I'm sorry I missed you."

"Yeah, sorry about that." Tessa was quiet for a few beats, then said, "I'm sorry about last night, too. The stress of this is getting the better of me."

"Me too." He pictured her twirling her hair the way she always did when she was uncomfortable. "It's not like you to leave work in the middle of the day."

Tessa sighed. "Just returning to the scene of the crime."

Biting the inside of his lip, Drew fought the urge to scold her for not being careful. "Did you come up with anything?"

"No. I was just checking to make sure I saw what I thought I did."

Several seconds ticked by before Drew responded. "You're not your mother, Tessa. Despite what might have happened in the past, you're a stable person. Just please don't go looking for trouble," he warned.

"Don't talk to me like I'm a child, Drew," Tessa warned gently. "I'm not looking for trouble. I'm just doing my part to make sure justice is done."

"I just don't want you doing something that will get you hurt."

He heard Tessa take a deep breath. "I won't. There have been some developments in the case, and the police are actively looking into it now. They've agreed to send a patrol car by my house every hour. They're looking out for me," she assured him.

"At least that's something," Drew mumbled, a gnawing feeling in his stomach. There was something she wasn't telling him.

"I need to get back to work. Thanks again for lunch. It was delicious," Tessa said, then disconnected the call.

Drew rubbed the back of his neck. Tessa could be infuriating. She was hardheaded, and when she set out to do something, nothing could make her back down. He just hoped the killer didn't find her.

A patrol car was something, but a lot could go wrong in an hour.

36

TESSA USED HER fork to cut off a wedge of chocolate cake and relished the bite.

Fear, she'd realized, had been robbing her of her life. Thinking back to the bird on the windowsill at Dr. Raymond's office, she vowed she wouldn't live in fear any longer. Not of the man who'd murdered that woman and threatened her, and not of the things others might do to hurt her.

She'd done her duty and reported a crime to the police, then had taken them the email this morning that proved not only that a crime had really occurred, but that she was in danger, too. They were sending a car by her house to make sure everything was okay, and within a few days, there would be a safe house waiting if she accepted their offer.

Sadness pierced Tessa's heart as she thought of the victim who set all this in motion. Did she have a family that was wondering where she was? Were they waiting for a dreaded phone call telling them she was dead?

Nobody should just be erased from the world, forgotten

for the sole reason that they hadn't been found. That couldn't happen to this girl.

There were enough imaginary monsters lurking around without a real one preying on young women.

After finishing the last bite of cake, she ran a hot bath and promised herself she would relax. Slipping into the water, she laid her head against the edge and closed her eyes, willing the warmth to ease the tension in her shoulders and back. Only losing Mama and her marriage falling apart had caused as much stress as this week.

Tessa began to drift to sleep but was jerked back into high alert by a loud scratching. She sat straight up, straining to hear where the noise was coming from.

Something, or someone, is in the house, her brain warned. She stood quickly and wrapped a towel around her dripping frame. She grabbed Drew's old baseball bat from her closet and moved slowly toward the noise. As she got closer, she realized it was coming from the living room.

I was just in there, she thought. There hadn't been anything there before I got into the bathtub.

Drawing the bat back, she stepped through her bedroom door and into the living room, ready to defend herself against the intruder.

Tessa's eyes searched wildly for the source of the scratching. She flicked on the light and looked again.

Nothing.

Taking a few cautious steps into the small room, she looked in the corner between the sofa and the wall. Again, nothing.

Still clutching the towel with one hand and grasping the baseball bat in the other, she inched toward the front door. Was something trying to get in?

Suddenly, the sound stopped.

Did I imagine it? she wondered, straining to hear the sound again. She shook her head. It was real. It had to be.

Dropping the bat, she placed a shaking hand on the knob of the coat closet inside the front door just as the scratching sound began again. She picked the bat back up, ready to strike, then twisted the knob and quickly pulled the closet door open. To her right were boxes she still hadn't unpacked even though she'd moved into this house a year ago. The boxes contained memories, mostly, and in her newfound independence she hadn't been in a hurry to relive the past.

She shoved aside one of the boxes and saw that there, wedged between two of the bigger ones toward the back, was a small electronic device. She didn't know how it got there, but she was certain in didn't belong to her.

Tessa picked it up, walked to the sofa, and sat down to examine it. It looked like a run-of-the-mill MP3 player, except this one had an alarm on it. She pressed play, and the sound of scratching pierced the silence. She adjusted the volume and continued to listen. It was almost as if the sound was playing on a loop, set to stop after a couple minutes.

He was in my house, she thought, panic erasing the calm she'd felt only minutes earlier.

How did he get in? He'd been there, going through her things, looking for just the right place to hide it.

Adrenaline coursing through her body, she stood, willing her knees not to buckle, and reached for the phone. She had to let Detective Jefferson know about this.

After hanging up, she rushed to her bedroom and threw on the first clothes she grabbed. She settled onto the sofa again, which gave her a view of every way someone could get into the house, and clutched the bat, ready to defend herself against the intruder.

Home wasn't safe. The police officer driving by every hour had missed the break-in, and it hadn't deterred the man who wanted to silence her.

Would she ever be safe?

Right now, it seemed like anybody's guess.

37

TESSA'S HANDS WERE clammy against the bat when there was a knock at the front door. Beads of sweat popped up all over her body.

She'd been unable to shake the feeling of having been violated. Someone had been in her house.

She pictured the dead, beady eyes searching for a place to put the device, his hands all over her things.

She shivered.

Tessa stood on shaky legs and walked to the front door. A glance through the peephole confirmed that there were two uniformed police officers responding to her 911 call.

Relaxing her grip on the bat, she opened the door and moved out of the way so they could enter.

"Everything okay here, ma'am?" the taller of the two officers asked.

"No. Nothing is okay here," Tessa said. She could feel her chest tightening and her breath becoming labored. The room began to spin; her arms went numb.

It had been months since she'd had a panic attack, but

considering the way the week had gone so far, she wasn't surprised that one was rearing it's awful head.

Through a constricted throat, Tessa managed to ask, "Is Detective Jefferson coming?"

The shorter, rounder officer nodded. "He's been made aware of the situation and is on his way."

She nodded, excused herself, then went to the kitchen for a glass of ice water. The cold always helped calm the panic.

When her breathing was a bit more regular, she rejoined the police officers. "What do you need?" she asked. Having to call 911 wasn't an everyday occurrence, and she wasn't exactly sure what to do.

"If you could tell us how you discovered your home had been invaded, we can start there."

Tessa retold the story, then pointed to the coffee table. "The playback device is over there."

The two officers exchanged glances. "You moved it?"

Swallowing hard, Tessa hesitated. The officers' nonverbal expressions weren't lost on her. "Well…yes. It was tucked between some boxes in the coat closet. When I realized what was making the scratching noise, I picked it up. I didn't think anything of it. Now, based on your reaction, I assume it was a mistake."

A movement at the front door caught Tessa's eye, and the officers excused themselves. She watched as Detective Jefferson walked into the house, then paused to talk to the uniformed officers. After a brief, muted conversation, Detective Jefferson nodded and walked toward her.

"Sounds like you've had an exciting evening," he remarked, glancing around the small house.

"Oh, yeah. It's been a real party around here," Tessa replied flatly.

The detective motioned toward the sofa. "Why don't you tell me about it."

Tessa followed him, then sat rigidly next to him as she recounted the discovery of the home invasion. "I'd gotten home from work late and was taking a bath. After a little while, I heard a noise. It sounded like something was scratching at the door. When I started looking around, I found this in my coat closet." She pointed to the device still sitting on her coffee table.

He pulled a handkerchief from his pocket and picked it up, turning it over to examine it from different angles. When he flipped the small switch, the sound of scratching penetrated the otherwise quiet living room.

"There must be some kind of alarm on it that made it start playing at a certain time, because it was absolutely *not* making that sound when I got home."

Detective Jefferson nodded slowly. To Tessa it looked like he was trying to process this new development and come up with a course of action.

"Someone must have broken in between patrols," the detective muttered to himself.

"Well, a lot can happen in an hour," Tessa said. Her voice was returning to normal, but even to her own ears, it still sounded strained.

"I'm afraid that's true," he agreed.

"But I don't know how he could have gotten into my house, or how he knows where I live." Her voice was rising again.

The detective leaned toward her. "We aren't certain who broke in."

"Who else could it be?" She wiped her hands on her lounge pants, stood, and began pacing around the room.

He stood with her. "I need you to think. Did you notice anything that seemed different anywhere else in the house? Maybe that something was out of place?"

Tessa stopped pacing and considered the question, then said, "No. Nothing."

"I'm going to have the house dusted for fingerprints and searched thoroughly to see if there are any other little surprises hiding here. Between this intrusion and the email you received this morning, I'm afraid staying here is the worst possible thing you could do. If this is the same guy, we already know what he's capable of. I would encourage you to accept our offer of a safe house. Unfortunately, you can't move in until tomorrow evening. Is there somebody you could stay with who will keep an eye on you in the mean-time?"

Tessa chewed her thumbnail, a subconscious move she always did when her anxiety was at its worst. "I don't know what to do…" she admitted. "There has to be something you can do."

For the first time since he arrived, Tessa noticed that the detective's broad shoulders were hunched even more than they had been this morning. The stubble on his face still hadn't been attended to, and his dark circles were even darker. This was a man who was exhausted and carrying more burdens than any one person should.

She'd heard rumblings around the news station that the police force was understaffed, but nobody reported it, and nobody dared tie the recent increase in crime to the fact that the mayor was cutting public service jobs to focus money else-where.

"I advise against you staying here, but if you insist, I can have a patrol car drive by every fifteen minutes," he offered. "I'm afraid that's the best I can do until the safe house is ready. I would really encourage you to stay with someone tonight. An extra set of eyes and ears certainly could help."

Tessa only nodded, knowing that if this guy knew enough to find her home and email address, there was a good chance she wouldn't be safe anywhere.

38

CRUMBS FELL ONTO his desk as Detective Al Jefferson took a bite of the ham and cheese on rye he'd picked up from an all-night deli after he left Tessa James's house. It wouldn't do anything to help his cholesterol, and if Darlene knew what he was eating, she'd have a fit.

He belched. His indigestion had nothing to do with the sandwich, and everything to do with Tessa James.

A veteran on the force, Al had spent the better part of his twenty-year career catching and locking up criminals. The other detectives acknowledged his expertise at reading suspects and putting together seamless cases that would lock up the bad guy. No one had questioned his ability in years.

Until this week.

He had to admit that he'd had doubts when the James woman first came to him. Even she'd had doubts about what she saw. Now she was in danger, and he was doubting himself.

He took a gulp of coffee and popped the last bite of sandwich into his mouth.

It wasn't easy, but he'd always done his job. For two

decades, he'd chased down every lead until the bad guy was behind bars.

This time was no different – except they had no proof to make a case.

The crime scene techs had done a thorough job dusting for prints and looking for fibers at her house, but they came up empty. They hadn't found a blasted thing that would tie the break-in to the creepy guy at the end of Oak Street. The cyber team hadn't fared any better. They couldn't identify the sender of the threating email Tessa had received that morning.

Not to mention that no one had found the body of the supposed murder victim from Monday night, and no matter what a witness saw, no judge would grant a search warrant with no evidence. His hands were tied, and he couldn't go outside the law to find what they needed.

He hadn't felt this helpless in a decade and a half.

Fifteen years ago, just after he'd made detective, he'd had a missing person case assigned to him. His first one. An eighteen-year-old high school senior named Kimberly Hamilton had gone missing after a movie with some friends.

She never came home.

In the weeks before her disappearance, she'd been fighting with her parents about extending her curfew, and her grades were steadily dropping. Mr. and Mrs. Hamilton called the police just one hour after she was supposed to be home, insisting that despite Kimberly's strong will and their frequent arguments, Kimberly would never have stayed out late without calling.

They insisted something terrible had happened to her, and what I saw was a troubled kid who took the curfew matter into her own hands, Al thought.

Though the arguments and problems in school pointed to a deeper issue, his gut nagged at him that it was something even more serious. Instead of acting on instinct, though, he'd gone through the spiel that it was a little too soon to report her missing. She was no longer a minor, after all. He'd obeyed protocol and waited until the next day to start looking into her disappearance.

Her body was discovered early the next morning in a garbage dump outside the movie theater.

She was just a kid, he'd reminded himself. No matter what, she was somebody's child, and I should have started looking right away.

Since then, he'd lived with the guilt that if he'd started looking into it when the parents called, maybe, just maybe, she would still be alive.

He vowed never to have another Kimberly Hamilton, and his gut, which was so often right, told him that if he didn't find something soon, Tessa James might meet the same fate.

Al wadded up the sandwich wrapper and tossed it into the trash can next to his desk, then drained the remainder of his now-cold coffee. He crushed the Styrofoam between his fingers and dropped it into the trash, too. Then he wiped his mouth with the back of his hand and pulled out the notes he'd taken at Tessa James's house.

Someone was daring enough to break into her house and plant something that would scare the pants off anyone while a patrol car was going by her house every hour. Also, he'd been slick enough to get access to her email address and smart enough to send a message that couldn't be traced. Even though he'd already gotten the name of the guy who lived in that house on Oak Street, there was nothing, other than Tessa's statement that indicated he might be involved. A background check showed he had no criminal record, not even a parking ticket. The guy was squeaky clean.

Detective Jefferson jotted a note: *Look into Tessa James's background.* Maybe he'd find a connection that way.

If it was the guy on Oak Street, why would he bother toying with her instead of just finishing her off? The email had warned her not to tell anyone what she saw. The man already knew she'd gone to the police, because Al himself, had visited him.

If he really had killed someone and intended to follow through with the threat he made to Ms. James, it was only a matter of time until he made his move.

Interrupting his train of thought, his partner, Detective Isaac Dunn, called from his desk, "Hey, Al, it looks like we've got a body!"

39

TESSA FLIPPED THE sun visor down to block morning sun as she drove back home from the news station. After snatching a few unsettled hours of sleep, she'd gone into work to rewrite the stories that had come in during the night. She'd gotten approval from Jack to do the rest of the rewrites from home, with the promise that she would get them done quickly. Old-fashioned to a fault, Jack was sure that anyone working from home was doing second-rate work. The only productive work, in his opinion, happened in the office while the employees were on the clock.

"I don't want you watching soap operas while you're working," Jack had told her, and he was still concerned, even when Tessa assured him she'd never watched a soap opera in her life.

Since she had been adamant that it wasn't Drew's job to take care of her, Tessa couldn't exactly go running to him last night once the police left. Instead, she dozed between dreams of a man, face contorted with maniacal rage, chasing her with a sheet of plastic clutched in his outstretched hands.

As she pulled up to her house, she was surprised to see Drew's car in the driveway.

What's he doing here? she wondered. After my blowup, he's the last person I expected to see.

She fiddled with her keys until she found the house key, making a mental note to get a locksmith over as soon as possible. If whoever was in her house last night had used the key she had hidden on her porch, she didn't want to give him that chance again.

Arms loaded with folders, and with one hand clutching her travel mug, Tessa inserted the key into the doorknob and turned it just enough to disengage the lock. She pushed the door open with her foot, and, still balancing her armload, kicked it shut.

Walking quickly to the kitchen, she dropped her stuff on the table with a relieved sigh, then whirled around at the sound of Drew's voice.

"I could have helped, you know," he said from the direction of the living room.

"How'd you get in?" Tessa demanded.

"You left your spare key just lying on the porch. Anybody could have let themselves in. You really need to be more careful, especially now," he scolded.

A shiver raced up Tessa's spine. "I didn't leave my key out. I keep it hidden in the dirt of the potted palm."

Concern flitted across Drew's face. "Are you sure?"

"Of course I'm sure." She looked around. "What did you do to my house?"

"I didn't do anything," he said, following her glance around the living room. "It looked like this when I got here. I assumed you just wanted a change."

Knees suddenly weak, Tessa lowered herself into the easy chair, which was on the opposite side of the room than it had been this morning. She buried her face in her hands and fought to take deep, controlled breaths. She could *not* have another panic attack right now. She needed to think.

Drew knelt in front of her. "Tess, what's going on?"

After another breath, she said, "It would seem that someone has broken into my house and moved all my stuff."

He stood and moved quickly around the small bungalow, checking the closets. "Nobody's here," he called from the next room. A few seconds later he was standing behind her, his hand protectively on her shoulder.

"I can't believe this is happening," she moaned. "I can't stay here."

His hands involuntarily squeezed her shoulder. "No. You can't."

"This is twice in under twenty-four hours," she said, desperately trying to keep her voice steady.

Drew's fingers dug harder into her shoulder. "What?"

As she explained last night's events, Drew's expression moved from concerned to angry. "Why didn't you call me?"

Ignoring the admonishment, Tessa said, "He's watching me. He has to be. How else would he have known I wasn't here? Unless he thought I was, and did this as a consolation prize."

"If that's the case, and he's gotten in here twice with the intent to kill, he's probably getting frustrated," Drew thought aloud. "That would only make him more dangerous." He turned back to Tessa. "You're not staying here. Go pack a bag. You're coming home with me," he commanded.

Tessa simply nodded and grabbed an overnight bag from the top shelf of her closet. As she packed, she couldn't stop thinking about that monster's hands all over her things. The sense of violation was overwhelming.

Once the overnight bag was packed, she scooped up the files she'd brought home to work on and they started toward the front door.

A knock stopped them in their tracks. Drew went to the door, looked through the peephole, and opened it.

The broad-shouldered man looked past Drew toward Tessa and said with a grim voice, "I think we found her."

40

AFTER THE INTRODUCTIONS, Tessa set a cup of coffee on the kitchen table in front of each of them and settled into a seat next to Drew. Clamping her hands around her own mug for several seconds before taking a drink, she hoped it would get rid of the chill she hadn't been able to shake all week.

"I'd like you to take a look at these photos and tell me if this woman bears a resemblance to the woman you saw Monday night," Detective Jefferson said, sliding a manila folder toward Tessa.

Tessa's stomach rolled. "Of course," she said, over the lump in her throat.

When she hesitated to open the folder, the detective reached across the table and did it for her, then arranged the photos in front of her.

She closed her eyes, trying to steel herself against the images that were about to be burned into her brain. As she'd learned when she found Mama, you can't unsee this kind of thing.

Willing herself to open her eyes, she glanced at the pictures of a young woman with wide, staring eyes. Each was taken from a different angle, showing just how unnatural the contortion of her body was. A mass of tangled hair framed her round face.

"It's not her," Tessa said and scooted the pictures away. She couldn't bear seeing another young woman, gone before her time.

Detective Jefferson frowned. "Are you sure?"

"Yes. This woman's hair is blond – much too light to be the woman I saw. Also, the woman in these photos would have been too heavy for the man I saw to hoist over his shoulder." Tessa looked back toward the pictures, her own eyes resting on the vacant, staring ones.

Was the face of her killer the last thing she saw?

Clearing his throat, the detective gathered the pictures and stuffed them back into the folder. "Thanks for taking a look. Looks like we're barking up the wrong tree with this one." He stood to leave, his shoulders slumping even more than they were when Tessa opened the door for him.

Tessa stood with him and said, "Detective, there's something you should know." After telling him that she came home to find everything in her house rearranged, and that Drew found the key laying out in the open on the front porch, she watched the detective as he processed the information.

"Ma'am," he began slowly, "you need to get out of this house immediately. The safe house will be ready later today. I don't want the next dead body to be yours."

"She's going to stay with me," Drew interjected. "I can protect her."

Detective Jefferson gave him a long look. "That's better than nothing," he said, disapproval heavy in his voice. "Keep an eye on her. It looks like this guy won't stop until he gets

ERIN LANTER

her." Disappearing through the front door, he left Tessa and Drew with the weight of knowing this guy would keep going until she was no longer a threat to him.

"Go finishing packing your bag," Drew told her. "I want you out of here. Now."

128

41

LOIS SIMMONS PULLED a loaf of sourdough bread from the oven and placed it on the cooling rack on top of her stove, keeping one eye fixed on the neighbor lady's house.

For someone who seems like such a loner, she sure has been having a lot of company lately, Lois thought.

The tall, handsome guy with the dark hair reminded Lois of a boy she'd gone to high school with. She'd had a crush on him all four years. The other man, who left by himself, looked like an aging football player whose body was starting to sag on him. The kind you could tell had been in good shape once but had let himself go.

In a quick motion, Lois slid a knife around the edge of the bread and released the loaf from its pan. She bent forward and inhaled deeply. Sourdough was her favorite.

She looked at the clock on the stove and counted how long she had to deliver this bread to Mrs. Oliver, a woman far too cantankerous for her age of forty-five.

"Maybe I have time to make another loaf," she mumbled

to herself. "A BLT would be delicious on this, and I know Walt would appreciate it."

She removed her starter from the refrigerator and went through the process of making a fresh loaf. Before long, the house once again smelled like baking bread. When the timer dinged, she quickly yanked the fresh bread from the oven, dumped it out on a cooling rack, grabbed the one that was wrapped neatly in cellophane, and dashed out the door.

As she was backing out, she caught sight of her neighbor carrying an overnight bag, a haunted look on her face.

"I wonder what's wrong with her," Lois wondered aloud.

Even though the only interaction she'd had with her neighbor was a quick chat at the mailbox, and she didn't really know her, Lois had the nagging feeling that something was wrong.

Pressing the gas pedal down harder, she made a mental note to keep an even closer watch on the house next door.

Just in case.

42

CARRYING HER OVERNIGHT bag into the house she'd called home until a year ago, Tessa realized how much she'd missed this place. It smelled different now, but still familiar – like Drew's spicy cologne and strong coffee. It was the first time she'd set foot in the house since the divorce, and she thought she was prepared for the emotions it would stir up.

She wasn't.

Tessa had never been the nostalgic type. Her childhood hadn't provided many memories to be nostalgic about. But now, standing in the house she and Drew had once shared, it overwhelmed her.

Drew came in behind her and pushed the door shut, engaging the deadbolt. It had been his nightly routine for a decade. The continuity was unnerving, almost like the past year hadn't happened. This time, though, he also walked around the house, checked the locks on every window, and ensured the back door was bolted.

"Welcome home," Drew said, dryly.

Tessa cringed. "Yeah, home," she muttered. She was a stranger in this house even though she knew it like her own face.

Drew picked up the overnight bag and led the way down the hall to the guest room. "This room is just how it's always been," he said, placing the bag on the armchair in the corner.

Tessa nodded. "I see that."

The soothing green walls and calming decor had been her way of adding balance to her life after Mama died. For several weeks after Tessa found her, she'd slept in the guest room so she didn't wake Drew up with her nightmares. During those weeks, she'd put her personal touches on the space, making it her own.

"I'm glad you're here," Drew said, taking a step closer, then stopping.

"Don't get used to it. I only agreed to this so you'd stop nagging me." Her sad smile communicated her failed attempt at humor.

The look on Drew's face mirrored her own.

It took every ounce of will power she had to keep her mind from wandering to the hideous possibility of what would have happened to her if she'd been home when that monster broke in.

A chill raced down her spine, and she visibly shuddered.

"I don't want you to be alone on the first floor, so I'll be sleeping right out there while you're here." He motioned toward the living room.

"No," Tessa protested. "That's too much. Giving me a place to stay that doesn't keep getting broken into is enough."

"It's not a suggestion, Tess. I'm sleeping out there." Drew's voice was firm and left no room for negotiation.

"My knight in shining armor," she said dryly.

He shrugged and walked to the door. With his hand on

the knob, he said, "I'm sure you want some sleep. You know where everything is. Goodnight."

When he was gone, Tessa unzipped her suitcase and grabbed her pajamas and toiletry bag. After a quick change, she washed her face and brushed her teeth, then pulled the covers back and sank into bed. Praying for a peaceful night, she drifted off to sleep. But the nagging thought at the back of her mind told her that the nightmare was just beginning.

43

TEARS ROLLED FREELY down Camille's cheek as she sat in the car, watching Drew's house. She fought to control her breathing, which in her mind was dangerously close to hyper-ventilation.

She was desperate to get back the feeling that Drew had given her of being worthwhile. Of course, sitting in her car outside his house wasn't part of her grand plan to get him back, but she hoped to at least get a glimpse of him. What she saw, though, was Drew moving on without giving her a second thought.

Her stomach dropped. "What does she think she's doing?" she groaned as Tessa walked through the front door carrying an overnight bag. "I can't believe he's doing this!" she wailed. "I've never been treated so shabbily in my whole life."

Of course you have, a little voice in her head reminded her. *But this is the first time it's ever hurt.*

She leaned forward across the passenger seat and squinted, trying to see what was going on inside. Parked across the street from his house, she didn't have a good view, but she could imagine.

Tessa had been reasonable when they spoke outside her house. Maybe she could plead her case again.

Slowly pulling out onto the road, she took one last glance at Drew's house.

"This isn't over," she vowed, and drove back toward her house and the bottle of wine she had on standby.

44

IT HAD BEEN another late night with not enough sleep. This was becoming the norm. Now, at six o'clock Saturday morning, Al Jefferson was at his desk again.

"There's not enough coffee on the planet to get me through this day," he muttered as he walked to the coffee maker across the squad room.

Most of the desks were still empty, leaving Al envious of his coworkers who were still asleep in their warm beds.

He lifted the pot and filled his mug, debating whether or not to just take the whole thing back to his desk. Nobody here needs it more than I do, he reasoned, then thought better of it. It would just get cold sitting on his desk. Once he got focused on a case, he usually forgot about the coffee anyway and ended up dumping most of it down the drain.

As he replaced the pot, he splashed some of the burning liquid on his hand and stifled the expletive that nearly escaped. Darlene hated it when he used bad language, and he'd been doing his best to watch his mouth.

Returning to his desk, he plunked his Cincinnati Reds

mug down and began making his to-do list. He'd learned early on in his career that he wasn't naturally organized enough to get everything done without one.

At the top of the list was getting Tessa James in to talk to a sketch artist. He needed to know what face she'd seen through the plastic. If they had any hope of identifying her, they needed to get at least a rough idea of what she looked like. Given the rain Monday night, and the distance Tessa was from the house, he knew a rough idea was all they could hope for. Also, since the home invasions seemed to be directly related to what she saw that night, he thought there was enough of a reason to invest a little more into the case, even though they still had absolutely no evidence.

Until she came in, though, the most pressing thing on the list was finding out what happened to the girl they found on the creek bed. The medical examiner hadn't gotten back with him yet about cause of death and they hadn't even established her identity.

He pulled out the file containing what little bit of information they had on the Jane Doe by the creek bed, then flipped through it and set it aside. It would have to wait until his partner, Isaac Dunn, got in. Until then, he had an hour and a half to satisfy his curiosity about Tessa James. There was something intriguing and oddly familiar about her.

He searched the criminal database and, to his relief, came up empty. Her fingerprints weren't on file and she'd never had so much as a parking ticket.

Then why do I keep feeling like there's a lot more to learn about her?

Just as he was about to give up, a memory came slamming into his mind. A couple years ago some of his colleagues had responded to a 911 call. There had been a suicide. A woman had found her mother hanging from the second-floor stair railing of her home.

What made me think of that case? he wondered. I wasn't even there.

He'd have to wait for Isaac for this, too. Isaac never forgot a name, a face, or a single detail from a case. He'd remember.

After all, just before he made detective, Isaac responded to the call.

45

TESSA STRETCHED AND looked around at the strange but familiar surroundings. Pulling the covers up to her chin, she sighed deeply, rolled over, and shoved her arm under the pillow. She hadn't slept that well since she moved into her own place, and it wasn't just because her second-hand bed and mattress felt like a slab of concrete. Her psyche remembered the night sounds and the gentle creaking of this house, and she'd been lulled to sleep in no time.

Finally resigning to get up, she dragged herself from the warmth of the bed. Life didn't stop just because it was the weekend.

Her stomach rumbled, reminding her that, in the commotion of the night before, she'd skipped dinner. This morning she felt like she could eat a whole herd of cattle. Or pigs. Pigs did seem to be the official breakfast animal, after all.

Without even taking a glimpse of herself in the mirror over the dresser, she opened the bedroom door and was greeted by the smell of her favorite breakfast.

Nearly tripping over a pillow and sleeping bag, she made

her way to the kitchen. Drew was standing by the sink in gym shorts and a rumpled T-shirt, sipping his coffee.

"Is that what I think it is?" Tessa asked, hope springing in her chest as she wiggled a finger toward the stove.

"Yep. Biscuits and gravy for the house guest." He put his mug on the counter and got two plates from the cabinet.

"You always were a terrific host," she said, saliva filling her mouth. She plucked three biscuits from the tray and broke them open on her plate. As she ladled the gravy over the biscuits, she said, "Why is there a sleeping bag and a pillow on the floor outside my room?"

Drew shrugged and looked away. "I told you I'd be right out here to keep an eye on you." He paused and rubbed his lower back. "I thinking I'm getting too old to sleep on the floor, though."

With a raised eyebrow, Drew watched as Tessa shoveled the food into her mouth. "You act like you haven't eaten in days."

"I missed dinner last night, and it's been ages since I've had biscuits and gravy. I fully intend to eat until I'm sick." Tessa got back to her breakfast, then looked back up at Drew. "I can tell you're judging me."

He just shook his head. "I was waiting for you, but it looks like you're in no hurry to return the favor."

"Then hurry up, will you? I'm going to get grumpy soon."

"We wouldn't want that," Drew said as he piled his own plate high with biscuits and saturated them with gravy. He took a seat across from her.

They ate in silence, but when Tessa's plate was half empty, Drew put his fork down.

Tessa looked up. "Are you done already?" she asked, still chewing.

"No. We need to talk." His voice was serious.

She pointed to her breakfast. "Don't ruin this for me, Drew," she warned.

"I don't intend to."

Tessa wiped her mouth with her napkin and set it on the table next to her plate. "Okay, then. What is it?"

"I really want you to be careful."

"You've already told me this." She started to pick up her fork, then paused. "I'm staying here so you can keep an eye on me. I'm being as careful as I know how to be. Unless I go to the safe house or end up in witness protection, this is as safe as it gets."

Tessa's cell phone rang. She hesitated, then went to the bedroom to get it and brought it back to the kitchen. "Hello?" she said, her voice wary. "I see… Yes, I'll be there as soon as I can."

She pressed the button to end the call and met Drew's questioning eyes.

"That was Detective Jefferson. He wants me to come to the station as soon as possible to meet with a sketch artist. He wants to try to get an idea about what the potential victim looked like, and he wants to double-check the identity of the guy I saw carrying her. Since there's no evidence, it wasn't necessary before. But he said that the break-ins at my house are too coincidental, and he wants to move forward with an investigation."

Drew watched her for a few seconds then said, "I'm coming with you."

"That really isn't – "

"I'm coming. I don't want you walking around out there by yourself. End of conversation," he said, his voice stern.

"Okay," Tessa agreed. She tried to take another bite, but suddenly the meal that had been so delicious just minutes before was now dry and tasteless. She scooted her chair back and took the uneaten food to the trash.

"I need to get dressed," she said, then went to her room and closed the door, leaning against it to take a few deep breaths. She certainly wasn't looking forward to recalling those dead, beady eyes of the killer, or the wide, staring ones of the victim.

The sketch artist's hand moved quickly as Tessa recalled the features of the young woman she'd seen wrapped in plastic. Try as she might, though, she couldn't recall enough detail to give him an accurate description. The finished sketch was general, at best. It could have been any woman between the ages of eighteen and thirty-five.

Describing the man was a different story. Her mouth dry, she described him feature by feature as the artist translated her words into an image that frightened her to look at. Drew, who'd insisted on accompanying her into the room, sensed her discomfort and placed a protective arm around the back of her chair.

When the sketch artist was finished, he spun the paper around and slid it over to Tessa. "Does this look right?"

Beads of sweat coated Tessa's forehead. She swallowed. "Yes. That's him."

Drew leaned closer and furrowed his brow. "Wait a second. This is who you saw?"

Tessa nodded. "Yes. Why?"

Even Detective Jefferson sat up straighter as he waited to hear what Drew had to say.

Frowning, Drew said, "It's just... I think I know this guy."

46

THE ROOM WENT silent.

"You know this man?" Detective Jefferson finally asked, urgency in his voice.

Drew nodded. "He's a new client."

"What can you tell me about him?" the detective pressed.

"His name is Jacob Armistead. I haven't been working with him very long, but he seems nice enough. Very backward, though. He doesn't make much eye contact, but he was polite. The only time he really opened up was when he talked about his work."

"Which is?"

"He's a psychiatrist and seems really passionate about it. The bulk of his work is in private practice, but I think he moonlights at one of the hospitals." Drew paused and looked at Tessa, whose wide eyes were unblinking. "When I first met him, I thought your mom might have benefited from someone like him."

Lowering her eyes, Tessa picked at a thread on her pants.

Regret throbbed in her chest. Nobody could have helped Mama. She didn't want help.

Detective Jefferson interrupted the moment. "So, he's a psychiatrist and your client. What do you do?"

"I'm a financial adviser. I work with people of high net worth."

"That would explain the guy's house," the detective muttered. "What else?"

Drew placed a comforting hand on Tessa's knee and gave it a squeeze before answering. "He's married, but from what I gather his wife travels a lot. She's in sales for a department store. Makes pretty good money. He didn't really talk much about her though."

Tessa's fear that she'd imagined what she saw dissipated. Someone else recognized the face. Even without the evidence the police needed to do a thorough investigation, more things were stacking up to convince them that, even though they hadn't found the body of the victim or any evidence that this man was the one who broke into her house, Jacob Armistead was far from innocent.

"In the interest of full disclosure, I will tell you that this man lives in the house on the end of the street, and I think it's time I paid him another surprise visit. Thank you both for your time. You've been very helpful." Detective Jefferson stood and picked up the sketch, studied it for a moment, then looked at Tessa. "We'll get him," he assured her. "These guys always slip up, and being seen by you was his first mistake. His second was having the case land on my desk." With that assurance, the detective stood and left the room. The meeting was over.

Tessa and Drew left, too. As they walked out of the police station, hope sprang up in her chest. It sounded like they might start making progress. With renewed energy, she walked toward Drew's car.

She hadn't imagined it. It had really happened.

Just because Mama was sick didn't mean Tessa was destined to be, too. As soon as this nightmare was over, she could finally start to live.

That man, who she now knew to be named Jacob Armistead, had killed that woman. She was sure of it. She was also beginning to think she wasn't the first person he'd murdered.

47

THE DOOR RATTLED in its frame as Al Jefferson pounded on it. Dr. Jacob Armistead hadn't necessarily been evasive on Wednesday, but he certainly could have been more forthcoming. At the time, Jefferson had still doubted Tessa and wondered what the good doctor had been hiding. Now he knew.

It was a stroke of luck that Drew James had accompanied Tessa to the meeting with the sketch artist this morning. Though he'd already done a check on the residents of that house, having the sketch confirmed by someone that knew him only strengthened his resolve to find out what happened in there Monday night.

His stomach clenched as an image of Kimberly Hamilton's lifeless body being hauled out of the garbage dump floated through his mind. Not taking a threat seriously was a mistake he'd promised himself he'd never make again.

Now he feared history was repeating itself.

He wasn't getting complacent in his work. In fact, Al considered himself far from crusty and jaded.

But he was tired. Tired of the long hours and the menial pay. When Tessa James came to report what she'd seen, it had been a rough day, and he hadn't been eager to go looking for a major crime to solve. The fact that no body turned up hadn't helped matters. He'd wondered if she'd been mistaken about what she saw. When they found the girl on the creek bed, he'd been certain they'd finally found the victim. But Tessa was emphatic that it was the wrong person, and that was the first time since he'd met her that there was no doubt in her voice.

Wind howled against the house. Even though it was a warm July evening, it chilled him. He turned the collar of his suit jacket up. He sensed a storm was coming.

Why isn't this guy opening the door? Al wondered. He pounded again. A car was parked out front, so somebody was home.

Finally, he heard footsteps approaching the other side of the door and the sound of a deadbolt disengaging. The door swung open and the same nondescript man he'd talked to the first time stood in front of him.

"Sorry to show up unannounced like this, but I have a few loose ends about that matter we discussed earlier that I need to tie up." Al did his best to keep his voice casual. His gut told him he needed to build some kind of camaraderie with the guy.

"Of course. Please come in." Dr. Armistead stepped back, allowing the door to swing wide open.

Al was greeted by spotless floors, neutral decor, and obviously expensive furnishings. Unlike the exterior, everything inside was just so. This guy was either a neat freak on steroids or had something to hide, and Al knew which one it was.

"Nice place you got here," he commented.

"Thank you. My wife decorated it herself. She's keeps wanting to start exterior renovations. That should take care of all the overgrown bushes and peeling paint. Frankly, I think it's ridiculous to spend that kind of money, but it made her happy. Besides, she's using money she inherited from a relative, so I don't have much say in the matter. In fact, she used that money to buy this house in the first place."

"I understand…" Al said. That fit with what he knew about this guy being a penny-pincher.

"Sorry it took so long to get to the door. I was in the middle of some paperwork and needed to get my notes jotted down while they were still fresh in my mind."

"Bringing the office home, huh?"

"In a matter of speaking, I suppose," the doctor replied. "I'm working on a book about conflicting delusions in individuals with paranoid schizophrenia. When something springs to mind, I have to write it down right away before I lose it."

Al grunted. "Sounds interesting."

"Oh, it is," Dr. Armistead said enthusiastically. "It's quite fascinating to see how mental illness manifests differently in each individual patient. Despite having the same diagnosis, all patients are unique. For example, two of my patients think they're God, and they had an altercation because they disagreed with the way the other created the world. Absolutely fascinating…"

Noting that the pulse in the man's neck quickened when he spoke about work, Al wondered whether this guy just got really excited about his job, or if he had a sick fetish about watching people squirm.

Finally returning to the present moment, the doctor said, "So, Detective. What can I do for you?"

Al took a moment to decide the best way to approach the topic. He wanted answers, but this guy had already skirted his questions once.

Gentle, he told himself. Make this guy think you're his pal.

"I was just wondering if you might have remembered something since I was here a couple days ago. You know how sometimes a memory just comes back to you."

Dr. Armistead shifted from one leg to the other and rubbed his hairless chin. Pursing his lips, he looked up at the ceiling as if trying to pull something from deep in his subconscious. He shook his head. "No, no, I don't think so. I'm sorry, Detective. If you'll recall, I answered all your questions when you were here Wednesday."

"Yes, I know, and I appreciate it," Al said kindly. "I do hate to ask you this, but would you mind coming down to the station to make your statement official? Then you can be done with me."

The doctor's voice rose in irritation. "I'm afraid I can't. As I already told you, I'm working on a book, and it's imperative that I write things down when they're fresh in my mind."

"I understand," Al said, trying to sound as agreeable as possible. "But you can understand my position. I have to cover all my bases so this witness will be satisfied I'm doing everything I can and finally leave me alone." On a hunch, he leaned closer, lowered his voice, and said in a conspiratorial tone, "You know how women can be."

A glimmer of understanding flitted across the psychiatrist's face. "Yes, I do. More than you know," he said with a smirk.

There's even more to this guy than I thought, Al mused. He doesn't seem to have a very high opinion of women. Makes me wonder about the wife. What kind of woman would marry this guy?

"You know, I've always thought this was a beautiful neighborhood, but I've never been inside one of the houses. Would you mind if I took a quick tour? Just to satisfy my girlfriend, of course. If she knew I was in one of these houses and didn't come back with all the details, she'd kill me." He winced inwardly at his choice of words.

"You don't have to tell her," Dr. Armistead suggested. "It's not any of her business where you go."

Whoa. This guy definitely has women issues, Al thought.

"Well, unfortunately for me, I don't have a dishonest bone in my body, and she can read me like a book. She'd know if I was keeping anything from her. Please? You know, just to keep the peace," Al asked again.

The psychiatrist huffed. "Fine. We need to make it quick, though. I need to get back to work."

"Thank you." Al followed the doctor's quick gait, making notes of his impression about the homeowners. Everything was immaculate. From what Al could tell, there wasn't a speck of dust or a single item out of place. Talk about highly controlled, he mused.

They walked quickly through the upstairs and were about to head back down when a room on the left caught Al's eye. Stopping mid-step, Al pivoted and walked in. Flipping the light switch, he gasped. "What the – "

A room full of nude mannequins greeted him.

"This is Samantha's room," Dr. Armistead offered, appearing from nowhere.

"Oh?" Al said. "Is she a seamstress?"

A high-pitched laugh escaped the doctor's throat. "Samantha? A seamstress? Definitely not. She's in fashion development but also sells new designs to major retailers. She often brings home prototypes and will dress the mannequins and fiddle with the clothing until it hangs just right. Then she reports the needed adjustments, and the company will fix them before she takes the new designs to retailers. Sometimes she carries these things around the house to see how the outfits look in different light. When she's being particularly absentminded, she forgets to put them back where they belong."

He sounded bored when he spoke about his wife's work but was thorough in explaining.

As though something suddenly occurred to him, Dr. Armistead snapped his fingers. "You know what? Samantha has been on a business trip and left a couple mannequins around the house. It's possible your witness saw me carrying one back upstairs."

Al nodded. The scenario made sense, but that wouldn't explain the threatening email Tessa received, or the fact that someone had been breaking into her house.

"Now, if you don't mind, I need to get some more writing done and then turn in for the night. I have to be at work early tomorrow."

"Of course." Making a mental note to check out Samantha Armistead, Al said, "I'll be in touch if I need anything further. Thank you for your time."

As Al opened the front door and stepped out onto the porch, he was greeted by a warm and gentle breeze, much different than the chill he'd felt just thirty minutes ago. Maybe there wouldn't be a storm, after all.

As he descended the steps and walked down the sidewalk to his cruiser, he wished that things had happened exactly how the doctor described, and that Tessa was mistaken about what she saw.

As he buckled his seatbelt, though, Al's gut told him that wasn't the case, and that the good doctor had a dark side.

48

THE SHRILL RINGING of the telephone woke Camille out of a fitful sleep. She rolled over and looked at the clock. Eight thirty.

She moaned, then grabbed her cell phone from the nightstand and glanced at the caller ID.

Beth.

"Do you know what time it is?" Camille asked groggily, flicking away a stray feather from her down comforter.

"Yes, it's time for you to be at work. Are you still asleep?"

"I was," Camille snapped, then pulled the covers over her head.

"You need to get moving, Camille," Beth urged. "You're going to get fired if you keep this up."

"I don't care," Camille whined. "Why do I have to work on Saturday, anyway?"

"Because all the relationship bankers have to take turns. You know that." Beth hesitated, then, with concern in her voice, asked, "Have you been drinking again?"

"What's it to you, *Mom*?"

"Watch it," her best friend warned. "I'm just trying to help."

"I don't want your help," Camille growled, then ended the call and tossed her cell back on the nightstand.

Her phone pinged, alerting her to a text message just as she pulled the covers back over her head.

She groaned. "What now?"

Picking the phone back up, she read the message several times, then sprang out of bed. She picked out her most flattering outfit and sky-high heels, applied her makeup to perfection, and spritzed on perfume. After fixing her sleek, honey-colored hair, she grabbed her purse and raced out the door.

If that text meant what she hoped it did, her life just might get back on track.

49

DETECTIVE ISAAC DUNN scraped the mud from the creek bed off his shoes, leaned back in the chair, and propped his feet up on his desk. Catching the Jane Doe case yesterday was the boost his career needed. With only two years as a detective under his belt, the more seasoned detectives still considered him a rookie. It was a title he was eager to shed.

He was as good at his job as almost anyone in the department, with the exception of his partner, Al Jefferson. At forty-five years old, Al's advice was sought by the other detectives any time they hit a snag.

His partnership with Al was pretty much non-existent these days, and it all started when that James lady came in to report a crime that no one could prove actually happened.

Usually, he and Al worked side by side, interviewing witnesses and possible suspects, but this time he hadn't shared any information with Isaac or bounced ideas off him. Despite his obvious exhaustion, Al just kept plugging along, keeping things to himself.

Isaac refocused his attention on the file in his lap. The

preliminary autopsy had come in, and according to the medical examiner, the Jane Doe from the creek bed was between the ages of twenty-three and twenty-seven. The external examination showed no sign of a struggle, but there were small puncture marks between her toes. The ME was still waiting on the results from the toxicology screen, but based on the location of the needle marks, drug overdose was a reasonable possibility as cause of death.

Death by overdose. An accident, right?

That's what they said about Marilyn Monroe, too. Though never one to put much stock in conspiracy theories, her case had fascinated Isaac long before he dreamed of being a cop. The idea that law enforcement might be involved in covering up a murder intrigued him. That a cop would cover up the truth, for any reason, blew his mind.

Even as a child, Isaac saw no gray areas. The whole world was painted in black and white, and anybody who tried to live in between ended up in trouble. There was no wiggle room where right and wrong were concerned, and while his friends at school were pushing boundaries, Isaac was holding steadfast to his personal code of ethics.

Typical firstborn, his parents had told him. Even they tried to get him to loosen up.

Isaac walked the straight and narrow, and that made him a good partner with Al Jefferson. Al, another black-and-white thinker, wouldn't ever compromise a case or sweep it under the rug because doing so was convenient.

But Isaac was afraid his partner had reached his limit this time.

What would happen then?

50

STILL REELING FROM her meeting with Detective Jefferson and the sketch artist, Tessa got out of her car and walked quickly across the parking lot. She had to keep her mind busy, and work was the only thing that would do that. She'd called Jack and asked if there were any weekend stories that needed rewritten. Jack assured her that there were and said he'd have them placed in her inbox.

Despite Drew's protests that she shouldn't go into the office to get them, she'd finally convinced him to make a pit stop at the office before heading home. With the promise that she wouldn't be long, he'd finally agreed to let her go into the building by herself, assuring her that he'd be watching to make sure she was okay.

She glanced over her shoulder and scanned the parking lot as the soles of her running shoes thudded softly against the asphalt. Listening to footsteps was becoming second nature.

In no mood for small talk and uninterested in getting yelled at by Drew for taking too long, Tessa sailed past the weekend receptionist with barely a nod and plunked her bag on her desk as she rifled through the stack of stories she had to rewrite. For once, she was glad to be confined to a cubicle. She didn't want to look at or talk to anyone else. Even under the best circumstances, Tessa had little tolerance for small talk. It was forced civility that proved most people were just putting on a facade. On a day like this, when her nerves were frayed and her buttons were just waiting to be pushed, meaningless chatter would be all it took to send her flying over the edge.

Her heart pounded as footsteps neared her cubicle. She dropped her head, hoping whoever was nearby wouldn't notice her.

The footsteps stopped right outside the flimsy wall that surrounded her desk. Reluctantly, Tessa looked up to see Emily, one of the station's best reporters, standing there with her chin resting on the top of the cubicle. Her hazel eyes danced with excitement.

"What are you doing here on a Saturday?" she asked.

"Just picking up some things to rewrite. I won't be here long," Tessa said, never making eye contact.

"What's up with you today? You're a little prickly. Get up on the wrong side of the bed or something?"

Tessa bristled. *Prickly?* If Emily only knew what she'd been through the past week, she'd understand why she was prickly. "I got up on the wrong side of the wrong bed, that's what happened," Tessa grumbled.

"Are you finally getting tired of sleeping alone? Cause if you are, I know this guy – "

"Not interested, Em. I stayed at Drew's last night."

"Ooh, I want details!" Emily whispered, looking around to make sure nobody else got the scoop on Tessa's juicy gossip.

Tessa rolled her eyes and shoved the papers into her tote bag.

"Did you two…"

Tessa stared daggers at her.

Emily tightened her lips then said, "Of course not. If you had, you wouldn't be so grumpy."

Tessa shook her head tightly. "I've gotta go. I'm working from home." She turned and walked toward the elevator, feeling Emily's eyes on her back until she rounded the corner.

Once outside, Tessa gulped the fresh air. She walked toward Drew's car, angry at Emily for insinuating anything had happened between her and Drew. What business of hers was it, anyway? She and Emily weren't even close friends. They were nothing more than office acquaintances.

"What took so long?" Drew asked once she was back in the car.

"Emily wanted to know why I was acting so prickly."

A soft chuckle scaped Drew's throat and a mischievous smile spread across his face. "Prickly? That's a new one. I might have to use that."

Tessa frowned. "Just drive," she muttered.

The two rode in silence until they reached Drew's house, then Tessa went into the guest room to check her email before she began retyping the stories.

Her throat closed.

The words "I'm watching" were in the subject line. The body of the email was completely blank.

The room began to spin.

I'm watching.

If he really is watching, he knows I'm not at my house. He knows I'm here with Drew, and neither of us are safe.

51

THE TENSION BETWEEN Detectives Jefferson and Dunn was noticeable, Isaac was certain of it. There was none of the usual banter that typified their partnership, just clipped comments and tight faces. Their responses to one another consisted of mostly primal snorts and grunts, making it sound like there were two animals in the squad room.

Isaac had decided that since Al was wrapped up in the Tessa James case, he'd take the initiative and be the lead in the Jane Doe case. He understood why Al was distracted, and he knew it all stemmed from the one screw-up he wouldn't ever forgive himself for – the Kimberly Hamilton case.

Any time a young woman went missing, Al was always paranoid he'd miss something that could lead to her being found. This time was no different, even though no one had even been reported missing.

In the past, Isaac had let it slide, but Al's behavior on this one worried him. He'd never put so much effort into a case with zero evidence.

Everything had made sense at first. Al looked into it, found nothing to support the witness's claims, and moved on. Or at least he tried to. For some reason, he was determined to ride a horse that wouldn't run. Isaac suspected there was something more personal about this case, something beneath the surface that wouldn't let Al move on.

Communicating in snorts and grunts wouldn't help. They needed to clear the air. Whatever was going on, Isaac was determined to get to the bottom of it so he could focus on clearing the Jane Doe case that was sitting on his desk.

52

AL WAS STILL in a foul mood. Despite being at his desk for the past three hours, he hadn't been able to nail down anything solid about Dr. Jacob Armistead.

His explanation about carrying a mannequin upstairs was a reasonable one, and Al had no problem with the logic of it. It had been raining that night, and Tessa's visibility would have been impaired. She hadn't been able to describe the victim, and it *was* possible that she'd seen him carrying a mannequin rather than a young woman.

So why did he keep digging?

Because she's had two home invasions and a threatening email, all of which happened after she saw him carrying something, or someone, over his shoulder, the voice in his head said.

Nothing added up.

A search on the good doctor, revealed that he was in private practice and charged a fortune to manage his patients' medication. He'd bounced around to different inpatient hospitals before going into private practice and doing part-time work inpatient work.

Al cocked an eyebrow. Why all the moving around? he wondered.

He looked up to see Isaac engrossed in the Jane Doe file. Then, shaking his head, Al picked up the phone and dialed.

"Judge Cooper," the man on the other end barked.

The judge was Al's old drinking buddy, and Al had kept enough secrets over the years to ensure Judge Cooper would be more than willing to do him a favor.

"Gavin, it's Al. How have you been?"

"Same old, same old," the judge said. "People still breaking the law and eating up taxpayer money. How's life treating you?" Even when he wasn't angry, Judge Gavin Cooper was brusque. Between his harsh voice and permanent scowl, he struck fear into everyone in the courtroom. Al didn't need to be afraid, though. He'd kept the judge's secrets.

Like the one about snorting coke with his mistress in Mexico when his wife was in the hospital with food poisoning.

"Same here. Listen, I wonder if you might do me a favor."

The silence on the other end was Judge Cooper's way of saying, "I'm listening."

"Well, I'm working on this case. Some things just don't add up. I've got a woman who says she saw a body wrapped in plastic being carried around this fancy house. Problem is, we don't have a body. No body, no crime, you know." Al paused for a moment in case his old pal wanted to interject. When he didn't, Al went on. "The thing is, this same witness has had her house broken into twice, and she's received a threatening email since then."

"What does that have to do with me?" Judge Cooper asked in his usual gruff tone.

"What I need from you is a search warrant." Al held his

breath waiting for a reply. He'd known before he made the call that it would be a long shot.

"You want a search warrant without evidence of a crime?"

"That's correct. You know I don't believe in coincidences." Al waited as the silence stretched between them.

At least he's thinking about it, Al thought hopefully.

"That's not really how we do things, Al. You know that," the judge admonished. "If you thought there was anything to this, you would have requested a warrant days ago to gather *fresh* evidence. Not evidence that's probably been destroyed."

"I know it's a little unorthodox, Your Honor, but I really think we need to get in that house to take a closer look," Al pressed.

"And you say there's no body?"

Al paused. "That's right." He felt his mouth droop. This was going nowhere.

The judge said, "I'll think about it."

The dial tone hummed in Al's ear. He'd done the best he could, but with no evidence to tie that psychiatrist to a crime, he knew there wouldn't be much he could do.

They needed to find that body. Without it, this case wouldn't go anywhere.

In the meantime, he picked up his pen and paper and walked to his partner's desk. It was time to find out if Isaac remembered anything about a suicide call a couple years ago.

As Al approached his partner's desk, he noticed Isaac's brows were furrowed in concentration. Without even looking at the file, he knew his partner was focusing on the Jane Doe case.

He had been all morning. Al was slightly perturbed that Isaac had taken over a case that had clearly landed on his own desk, but he had to admit that he'd done the same thing with Tessa James and the maybe-murder.

"Hey, Isaac. How's it going?" Al tilted his head toward the open file laying on the desk.

"Fine. We're getting closer to having her identity. It's tricky, since there was no identification on the body and nobody has reported her missing, but we'll get there. I'm hoping her fingerprints are in the database. That would be the best-case scenario." He paused and studied Al. "What's up?"

"I had a question about a suicide call you responded to a couple years ago, just before you made detective."

"Unfortunately, we get a lot of those calls," Isaac said as his fingers clicked the keyboard. "Do you have any details that will help me out?"

Al looked up at the ceiling. "It was two, maybe two and a half years ago. A woman. Not really elderly. Late fifties, early sixties, maybe. Her daughter found her hanging from a banister in her stairwell and called 911."

Detective Dunn's fingers stopped typing. He looked up at his partner. "I remember that one. It was just before I took the detective exam." He paused and shook his head. "That was a tough one. The daughter was a mess, almost hysterical. She claims she saw a man running away from the house when she got there and made some noise about him maybe killing her mom. There was no evidence to support that, and once we ruled it a suicide, she calmed down a bit. It was sad. She didn't even seem surprised, almost like she expected it to happen."

"Oh? Why was that?" Al's internal radar was onto something.

"The mom had been struggling with mental illness for decades. Really paranoid, imagining things that weren't there. I think the daughter said she had schizophrenia or something, but that she refused to get help. The impression I got was that the daughter felt she was responsible for taking care of her mom." Isaac shook his head. "What a terrible way to live."

"Do you happen to know the name of the victim?"

Isaac's fingers tapped the keys again. Al watched as his eyes moved back forth as he read the report he'd just pulled up. His intuition again told him he was onto something.

"The victim's name was Anita Wells."

Al took a deep breath. "And the daughter's name?"

"Let's see..." Isaac's eyes tracked the words again. "Looks like the daughter's name is Tessa James."

Al pressed his lips together, then, as the phone on his desk began ringing, said, "That's my witness. Looks like she has a history of imagining crimes that never happened."

53

TESSA FROWNED AND pressed the button to disconnect her call. That was the coldest Detective Jefferson had ever been to her. He sounded almost skeptical when she told him about the newest email threat.

Is it just fatigue? she wondered. Why would he stop believing me now?

Again, she felt like it was up to her to keep herself safe. Sure, Drew was there, but things couldn't go on like this. If that monster really was watching her, he'd know she was with Drew, and Drew would be in danger, too.

She couldn't stay here. Unless the offer of a safe house was still good, there was nowhere she could go.

He was watching her, and she was certain he intended to kill her. So why was he toying with her?

Tessa shuddered.

Her gut told her that the game was almost over.

54

CAMILLE LOOKED OVER her shoulder and slipped the key into the lock. Hidden by the shadows, she twisted the knob and slipped noiselessly inside. She groped the walls on each side of her, searching for the light switch.

This wasn't how she typically spent a Saturday night, letting herself into an ex-boyfriend's ex-wife's house, but the text had been clear.

It's Tessa. I think we should talk. Come over to my place around 7:00 tonight. If I'm not home, use the key buried in the flowerpot to let yourself in.

Her fingers found a switch, and when she flipped it on the room was illuminated in a warm glow. Blinking at the light, she allowed her eyes to adjust and walked into the living room. She slipped the key in her pocket and sat on the sofa.

She placed a hand over her mouth to stifle a yawn. Her afternoon mai tai to celebrate what might happen when she and Tessa talked tonight had left her drowsy.

If she didn't get up and move, she was going to fall asleep

on Tessa's couch. That wouldn't leave a very good impression, would it? she told herself.

Deciding it couldn't hurt to look around, Camille began moving through the small house. Just as she was about to walk down the short hallway toward the back of the house, she heard a thump from what she assumed was the bedroom. A scraping sound followed, then she heard a click.

Goosebumps pricked her spine. She wasn't alone.

Is Tessa in there? Why didn't she come out earlier? Certainly she must have heard me, Camille thought.

Her curiosity outweighed her fear, and she inched closer to the bedroom door. Just before she reached for the knob, the door flew open. Frozen in fear, she couldn't run or scream.

Her heart beat wildly as two shots rang out, then Camille's body crumpled to the floor.

55

EARLY SUNDAY MORNING, Lois Simmons was already busy in her kitchen. She'd run behind on her customers' orders and hadn't gotten to the pound cake she wanted to take to her neighbor.

"I feel so bad," she'd lamented to Walt. "How could I have let this happen? I was supposed to take my pound cake to her on Friday."

Walt sat at the kitchen table, reading the newspaper and drinking his coffee. "She didn't even know you were planning to make one for her. No harm in being late, I say."

"But Walt," she'd protested, "I made a commitment. If I'm going to be this lazy, how can I possibly keep my home-based bakery afloat?" Worry lines creased Lois's otherwise flawless face.

Walt lowered the paper and studied his wife. "Lois, dear, you're anything but lazy. You haven't come to bed before midnight a single night this week because you've been filling orders," he soothed. "I'm proud of how hard you've been working."

Lois beamed at him. Even with flour on the tip of her nose, she knew Walt still thought she was a beauty.

The egg-shaped timer that had been a wedding gift all those years ago buzzed.

"Ah, it's done." Lois grabbed her oven mitts from the drawer next to the stove and opened the oven door. She inhaled the intoxicating fragrance of warm blueberries and sugar as she pulled the pound cake out of the oven. "Perfect," she announced as she slid it onto the cooling rack on the counter.

"How could it be anything but?" Walt said as he raised the newspaper again.

"Oh, Walt. You encourage me so…" Lois said wistfully.

After putting the finishing touches on a few more orders, Lois wrapped the pound cake in a cellophane bag and tied it with a ribbon. "I'm going to drop this off next door," she said as she slid her feet into her orthopedic flip-flops. "And maybe I'll get the scoop on the man who's been hanging around there this week."

Walt grunted in agreement. Lois knew he didn't care about their neighbors' personal lives but appreciated that he at least pretended to listen.

"By the way," Lois said, fluffing the ribbon one last time. "Did you hear anything last night? It sounded like somebody's car backfired a couple times."

"No, I didn't hear anything," Walt said absently. "You always say I sleep the sleep of the dead."

Lois shrugged. "Oh, well. I'll be back in a few minutes."

She walked outside into the warm morning sun and turned her face up to the sky. Stuck in the kitchen all day, she didn't get to enjoy the outdoors as much as she would like.

After walking the two dozen or so steps that separated

their homes, Lois climbed the stairs to the porch. She frowned. Tessa's car wasn't there, but the front door was open a crack. "Hello?" she called, nudging it open a little more. "Anybody home?" Another nudge.

Lois squealed as a bird flew toward her. "What in the world?" she muttered, then walked carefully into the house. She didn't want to get arrested for trespassing, but something just didn't feel right.

"Hello? Anybody here?" she called again.

She took a few steps into the living room and stopped. Her eyes rested on a motionless figure on the living room floor.

"Sweet baby Jane!" she gasped and rushed toward the woman. She dropped the pound cake and squatted next to her.

Lois could tell she was breathing, though faintly. She sprang to her feet and looked around wildly for a phone.

"Why doesn't anybody have landlines these days?" she snapped, then turned back to the woman on the floor. "I'm going to call 911. Help will come!" she yelled as she raced out the door to her own house.

That woman certainly wasn't her neighbor. What was that poor thing doing getting herself shot in someone else's home? Lois thought as she burst, panting, through her kitchen door and flung herself toward the phone.

56

LEANING AGAINST THE door frame, coffee still in hand, Dr. Jacob Armistead scanned Samantha's home office. For once, her silly career in fashion had benefited him.

She did always look gorgeous, though. The few times she'd accompanied him to social events, his friends and colleagues had commented on how beautiful she was. The men always said they wished their wives took care of themselves the way Samantha did. He never mentioned that she was at least a full decade younger than anyone else in the room.

In his opinion, none of it mattered anyway. Only the least intelligent people put so much effort into their appearance. Many times throughout their six-year marriage, he'd wondered how they'd ended up together. Of course, she'd managed to hide her least desirable qualities until after they were married. Typical woman.

The number of times they'd fought about these stupid mannequins... he'd been ready to call it quits. Now they'd finally come in handy. Perhaps he shouldn't complain about them so much in the future. They had, after all provided him with the perfect explanation of what happened Monday night.

He groaned as the phone rang. "I sincerely hope it's not that nosy detective again," he muttered as he wove between the half-naked mannequins to answer the phone on Samantha's desk.

"Hello?" he said with forced pleasantry while flipping through the sketchbook containing his wife's ideas for a new clothing line. Even though her specialty was sales, she had an obvious talent for design.

This explains all those long hours she's been spending in here, he thought.

"Hi, J!" Samantha's enthusiastic greeting grated on his nerves.

Why can't she manage my whole name? It's not a difficult name to pronounce. Just say it. He clenched his teeth and asked, "How's your trip?"

"Absolutely terrific! I sold one of my own designs to Bloomingdale's. Can you believe it?" she gushed.

"That's wonderful," he said, continuing to flip through her sketchpad.

"Isn't it? They bought the knee-length cobalt dress with the asymmetrical hem and peasant sleeves. I thought I was taking a gamble showing it to them, but they loved it. I guess that's proof we should always trust our instincts, isn't it?"

"Mm-hmm," he agreed absently.

Near the back of the sketchbook, he came across a sketch of a bright blue dress with flowing sleeves and an uneven hem. Is that what Bloomingdale's bought? It's ghastly.

"And even better news," Samantha continued, "is that I get to come home early."

He snapped to full attention. "What?" he croaked.

"I get to come home early," she repeated. "My meetings went quicker than I thought, so I don't have to stay here another two days. When I get home, we'll celebrate!"

"I couldn't be happier," he said, slamming the book shut. "What time will you be back?"

"I'm taking the red-eye home tonight. My flight lands at four twenty-six tomorrow morning."

His mouth went dry when he checked his watch. Nineteen hours until she touched down. He picked up the mug he'd set beside the phone and took a final gulp of coffee, forcing it over the lump in his throat. "That won't give me much time to get things ready for a celebration," he said, laughing nervously.

"Oh, J," Samantha said tenderly. "I'm so glad you're happy for me. I know you sometimes think what I do is silly, but it means so much to me that you want to celebrate. I'm finally doing what I've always wanted to do."

A momentary stab of regret pierced his stomach. Samantha really was a sweet woman, and a striking beauty with jet-black hair that flowed halfway down her back, large brown eyes, and perfectly symmetrical features. "I'm proud of you, Sam. You've worked hard for this, and I'm glad it's finally happened for you." He paused. "What should we do to celebrate?"

"Maybe a nice dinner, a bottle of wine, and a huge slab of chocolate cake."

His eyebrows shot up at the last request. Samantha had an iron will when it came to what she ate, always saying she liked looking good in her clothes more than she liked any food on the planet. He chuckled. "Consider it done. I'll find the biggest, richest, most delicious cake in town."

"Good," she agreed. "I need to get ready for my meeting

this morning. I'll call you before I get on the plane. I love you, J."

"You, too," he murmured, his palms suddenly slick with sweat.

He looked at his watch. He had exactly ten minutes to finish getting ready for work, but that was the least of his problems right now. In the midst of his busy day, he had to figure out where to hide the body that had been stuffed in the chest freezer in his garage all week. He only had nineteen hours to erase any evidence he might have left behind.

57

"JUST ANSWER THE question, Ms. James," Detective Jefferson demanded. "Do you own a forty-five-caliber pistol?"

Tessa's head was spinning. This can't be happening, she thought. Having a police detective show up at the front door to question her about a gun she'd bought a year ago and never used was the last thing she expected today. Of all days for Drew to decide to go into the office.

"Yes, I do. I bought it shortly after my divorce."

"And what was your intention when you bought the gun?" he prodded.

"Protection," she said, trying to wrap her head around what Detective Jefferson might be implying. Why did her gun suddenly matter?

"Did you think you needed protection from anyone in particular?"

She cut her eyes to the younger detective, who so far hadn't said anything. Detective Jefferson had introduced him as Detective Dunn. "No," she said. "When I started living by myself, I felt like I needed a little extra security. I don't exactly live in the best neighborhood."

Tessa remembered the day she bought the gun like it was yesterday. She'd walked into the gun shop, picked out the one she wanted, and paid cash. The purchase had made a big dent in her savings, but with it she felt more prepared to handle the world and its unknowns. After filling out the necessary paperwork, the clerk had handed the gun over immediately.

"There's no waiting period?" she'd asked, taken aback.

The clerk's words were, "Nope. Welcome to the south ma'am."

At that moment, she'd become a gun owner. Aside from the few trips to the shooting range to familiarize herself with the weapon, she hadn't given it another thought.

Detective Jefferson changed directions. "Okay. Let's talk about Camille Walker."

"What about her?"

"How well did you know – " Detective Dunn began. His partner didn't let him finish.

"What was your relationship to her?"

Tessa squinted into the sun streaming through the living room window. "There wasn't one. I met her once last week for about five minutes. Why?"

"And what were the circumstances of your meeting?" Detective Jefferson asked, pulling his notepad out of his breast pocket.

"She was poking around outside my living room window," Tessa offered.

"What do you think she was doing?" Detective Dunn asked.

Before she could answer, Detective Jefferson interjected, "Someone was spying on you through your living room window, and you didn't think to tell us? After what you witnessed?"

"I wouldn't call it spying. She just wanted to talk." Tessa's eyes moved back and forth between the two detectives.

"I don't suppose you know why she'd come to your house, a total stranger, *just to talk.*"

Tessa sighed. "She'd been seeing my ex-husband. He broke it off one afternoon, and that evening she came to my house. Apparently she had it in her head that we were getting back together and wanted me to know she wasn't giving up."

"Seeing someone outside your window must have been frightening," Detective Dunn empathized.

Tessa nodded.

"Would you say you felt threatened by her? Like maybe you needed to defend yourself?" Detective Jefferson challenged.

Tessa tilted her head. "I've been more than cooperative in answering your questions, Detective. Would you please tell me what this is about? I think you owe me that courtesy."

"One of your neighbors found Camille Walker shot in your home early this morning."

Tessa blinked. "I'm sorry. Did you just say that Camille was shot in my house? What was she doing there?"

"I was hoping you'd tell me, Ms. James."

Tessa's eyes tracked a boy riding his bicycle down the street. "This is why you've been asking about my gun? I haven't shot it in months."

"The evidence disagrees with you, I'm afraid. We found a forty-five lying next to her body. It's being checked for fingerprints and residue as we speak."

"Camille was shot in my house? *Maybe* by my gun?" Tessa

asked. She had the strangest feeling that she was floating above her body. "That's impossible."

Detective Jefferson stood. "I'm afraid it looks like it's very possible, and that you're the most probable suspect."

"But I'm not even staying there!" Tessa protested. "In case you've forgotten, someone has broken into my house on at least two occasions. *That* is the person who probably shot her."

Just before he walked out the door, Detective Jefferson turned to her and said, "Ms. James, if you're the praying type, you'd better start begging God to let her live. Otherwise, you might find yourself facing a murder charge."

"But I had no reason to want her dead," Tessa called at the detective's retreating back.

As the cruiser drove away, she wiped the sweat from her forehead and took deep, calming breaths in attempt to regain her equilibrium.

They didn't arrest me. At least that's something, she reminded herself.

If she didn't know any better, she'd think somebody knew all her worst nightmares, and, over the past six days, was forcing her to live them one by one.

58

CLENCHING HER TEETH against the shaking, Tessa walked through the kitchen and into the garage, where Drew had insisted she park her car to keep it out of sight. He'd made her promise to stay put and not try to go anywhere while he was at the office, but these were extenuating circumstances. He needed to know about Camille, and it couldn't be done on the phone.

Never in a dozen lifetimes would she have imagined she'd be a suspect in a shooting.

This is all so absurd, she thought angrily. I wasn't even home. I've been staying at Drew's.

The fact that Camille had been shot *inside* her home didn't look good. She'd known that before Detective Jefferson even pointed it out. Somehow they'd turn this into a crime of passion.

What was she doing in my house? How did she get in? Tessa wondered, then remembered that it must not have been very hard, considering this wasn't the first – or even second – time someone had broken in this week.

As the questions tumbled around in her head, Tessa had the sinking feeling that whatever had happened to Camille was intended for her.

Of course it was. How could the police believe anything different? Nothing like this had ever happened until I went for that blasted walk and saw what that psychopath was doing.

Tessa's stomach churned. How could Detective Jefferson really believe she shot Camille?

She turned her car toward Drew's office. What will he think? Tessa worried. Surely he'll know I wouldn't do something like that. Besides, he knows I was at the house all night.

Right?

A new wave of panic swept over her. After she picked up her work from her office and got the threatening email, she'd holed up in the guest room to work. The only time she'd come out was to get a pizza she'd ordered from the delivery guy. She didn't know if Drew slept on the floor outside her room or not. Avoiding him as much as possible seemed to be the best way to protect him if that awful man really was watching. Unless he'd slept on the floor outside her door again, he'd never know if she slipped out during the night. For all he knew, she could have gone to her own house, shot Camille, and sneaked back in without him ever knowing.

Even if he was outside the door, he'd always been a heavy sleeper and she could have easily crept around him.

Once in the parking lot of Drew's office building, she parked, quickly glanced around, then ducked her head and walked inside.

Tessa tensed when she saw Dorothy sitting dutifully at her desk.

What is she doing here on a Sunday? Tessa wondered.

"You can't go in there," Dorothy said, an air of authority in her voice. Dorothy loved Drew like an overprotective mother would. After the divorce, she had been vigilant about looking out for him. Now the evil ex-wife was there to wreak havoc on Drew's life, and Dorothy was ready to defend him.

Tessa turned and smiled. "Hi, Dorothy. How are you?" Tessa was surprised how civil she sounded. She'd never liked Dorothy.

Dorothy scowled at her. "What do you want with Drew?"

Tessa's smile fell. What business was it of hers what she wanted with Drew? "I just need to talk to him."

"He's in a meeting and can't be disturbed," Dorothy said coldly, then turned her attention back to a stack of papers on her desk.

Tessa looked toward Drew's office. The door was open, and he was sitting at his desk, alone, eyes fixed on the paper he was holding.

She took a step toward his office only to be scolded by the overbearing assistant. "I told you he's in a meeting," she growled.

Tessa was sure no wolf was more intimidating than the woman behind her. She turned to face her. "You know, Dorothy, that would be a lot more convincing if the whole front wall of his office wasn't glass." She turned and took several steps toward Drew's office, Dorothy hot on her heels. Tessa tapped lightly on the door frame.

Drew looked up, surprise and annoyance registering on his face. "Tessa, what are you doing here?"

"I'm so sorry, Mr. James," Dorothy said breathlessly. "I tried to stop her, but she wouldn't listen." Dorothy stared daggers at Tessa.

A smile tugged at the corner of Drew's mouth. "That's quite all right, Dorothy. Thank you."

Dorothy snorted and walked away, dropping heavily into the chair behind her desk.

"I can't believe you overpowered the palace guard," Drew said, chuckling.

Tessa shook her head and hooked her thumb over her shoulder. "I wonder how she's going to replay *that*."

Drew shrugged. "I don't know, but if you stick around, I bet you'll find out. I'm sure it will be an Academy Award-winning performance," he said, laying the papers on his desk and intertwining his fingers. "What was so important that you were willing to go toe to toe with Dorothy? Not to mention the risk of that guy following you. You promised you'd stay home and keep a low profile," he scolded.

Tessa took a shuddering breath and sat in the chair on the opposite side of Drew's desk. "I'm in trouble, Drew."

"More trouble? What's with you these days?" he asked. Tessa wasn't sure if he was trying to be funny or if he was genuinely upset.

Tessa dropped her eyes and twisted her hands together. "It's Camille. She's been…shot."

Drew sank back in the chair as though the wind had been knocked out of him. "Shot? You can't be serious."

Tessa nodded.

"Who would want to hurt Camille?"

"I don't know. The police just questioned me at the house. I assume they'll be trying to contact you soon."

Drew went quiet. When Tessa finally looked at him, he was staring straight ahead, shaking his head. "This can't be happening." He rubbed his face, suddenly looking as if he hadn't slept in a week.

"I'm so sorry, Drew," Tessa said quietly. It was obvious Drew had really cared about Camille.

He pulled his gaze away from whatever he'd been staring at and looked at her. "Wait a minute. You said you were in trouble. How does Camille getting shot have anything to do with you?"

She didn't say anything.

"Tessa, what's going on?" Drew urged.

"She was shot at my house. Apparently it happened last night."

"Your house? What was she doing at your house?"

"I don't know. I've been wondering the same thing." Tessa wrapped her arms around her torso and added, "I think the police think I did it."

"You? Why would they think you did it? You don't even have a gun."

Tessa dropped her eyes to her lap. "Actually, I do," she admitted.

"Since when?" Drew asked, incredulous.

"Since we got divorced and I've had to live by myself in an undesirable part of town," she said, then rolled her eyes up to the ceiling and exhaled. "I don't even like guns. I only practiced with it a few times."

Drew ran his fingers through his hair. "What's going to happen to you?"

Tessa shrugged and splayed her hands out in front of her. "I don't know. Detective Jefferson just questioned me at the house. He said they're running some tests on the gun to see if mine is the one that shot her. I guess depending on what comes back, I'll either be in the clear or up to my eyeballs."

Drew shook his head tightly. "That's ridiculous. You'd never hurt anybody."

"I know. I'm afraid my having a gun might give the police a different impression, though."

"Well, you couldn't have done it anyway. You have an alibi. You were at my house all night. I can testify to that," Drew offered.

"Can you?" Tessa challenged.

"What are you talking about? Of course I can."

"And when was the last time you saw me?"

"About seven. When you got your pizza from the delivery guy." His eyes widened. "You were in your room all day. But I was in the house all night, and so were you."

"I could have sneaked out, you know. Done the deed, then been back before you realized I was gone."

"Oh, please. That's ridiculous. There's no way you left my house, drove there, just happened to find Camille in your house, shot her, and came back pretending nothing happened. There's no way." Drew shook his head emphatically.

"I know that," Tessa agreed, "but I don't think Detective Jefferson is going to see it that way. If results show that my gun was the one used to shoot her..." Tessa looked at Drew in anguish. "I'm in big trouble."

59

CAMILLE BLINKED AGAINST the bright lights shining above her. Where am I? she wondered.

As she regained consciousness, pain shot through the right side of her stomach. She groaned. A nurse was immediately by her side.

"Welcome back, Ms. Walker. How are you feeling?" the nurse asked in a cheerful tone that annoyed Camille to her core.

"Just peachy," she answered sarcastically.

"We have someone here who would like to see you. Would you be up for a visitor?"

Hope sprang up in Camille's chest. "Yes, of course."

"It will be just a few minutes," the nurse said, then turned as she walked from the room.

Panic replaced the hope she'd been feeling only moments before. Though she had no mirror, Camille was certain she looked awful. After quickly wiping her eyes, she slapped her cheeks and ran her fingers through her hair. That was the best she could do.

She pushed the call button. After what seemed like forever, the nurse reentered the room.

"Can I get something for the pain? I feel horrible."

"Right away, Ms. Walker. You're due for another dose, anyway." The nurse disappeared as quickly as she'd come.

Right away my foot, Camille fumed.

She huffed and wondered who was there to see her. She had no family and only a few friends.

Then, sighing happily, she realized it could only be one person. Deciding she could make her appearance work in her favor, she shrunk down further in the bed and tilted her head to one side, forcing an expression of misery onto her face. Not that it was hard when she felt so awful.

At the light knock on the door, she turned her head expectantly.

"Hi," the visitor said softly. "How are you feeling?"

Camille's hope was dashed. "Oh, it's you."

"It's nice to see you, too," Beth said.

"I was hoping you were Drew," Camille complained.

Beth spread her arms. "What gave me away?" she asked lightly, then her tone turned serious. "What happened to you?"

Camille shook her head. "I don't know."

"You have no idea?" Beth asked, surprise in her voice.

Camille shrugged against the pillow.

Beth hesitated a moment. "Nobody has talked to you about what happened?"

"No. They said something about a shot, but no one has given me any shots. Just this IV," she said, pointing to her right arm, "but I don't think that counts. They only told me I lost a lot of blood and have anesthesia or something, so I can't remember anything."

Beth coughed into her hand to cover her laugh. "You mean *amnesia*?"

"Yeah, that. Don't make fun of me. I think these pills are making me loopy."

Just then, the nurse returned with a small cup of water and a pill Camille figured must have been a horse tranquilizer. She popped the pill in her mouth and chased it with the shot-glass sized cup of water, nearly choking as it went down.

"Aren't I on some kind of schedule? This was supposed to be here a while ago." Camille closed her eyes and rested her head back against the pillow.

The nurse narrowed her eyes at Camille, and without saying a word, left the room.

"Is she gone?" Camille asked.

"Yes."

"Good. These nurses are so annoying," she muttered. "Where were we? And be quick. Whatever they gave me will knock me out cold in just a few minutes."

Beth smirked. "We were talking about your anesthesia."

Camille opened her eyes and shot Beth a withering look.

Beth cleared her throat. "Sorry. We were talking about what happened to you." She lowered her voice. "Camille, you were at Tessa James's house. And they aren't going to *give* you a shot, you *were* shot. With a gun."

Camille raised her head off the pillow. "She shot me?" At once the drowsiness was gone. "Figures," she mumbled.

"I don't know who shot you, Camille. Did you see anybody?" Beth urged.

Camille shrugged. " I don't know. It happened really fast."

"Please take this seriously, Camille," she ordered. "You

were the victim of an attempted murder. You've got to figure it out. Fast."

Nodding in agreement, Camille thought a moment, trying to force any snippets from the night before into her memory. She vaguely remembered having a key in her hand. There had been a noise, and she'd gone to check it out. A door opened, and someone had been standing there with a gun. She didn't remember the face. That part was fuzzy.

It could have been Tessa.

It could have been anybody.

60

BACK AT THE station, Isaac Dunn slammed the folder he was holding onto his desk.

"What crawled up your shorts?" Al asked.

Isaac answered with a cold glare.

"What?"

"What was that when we were talking to the James woman?" the younger detective demanded.

"What was what?"

"That," he said, pointing to the general direction of outside. "You wouldn't even let me talk."

Al shook his head. "I was questioning a possible suspect, just like we've done dozens of times."

Detective Dunn crossed his arms over his chest. "No, Al. That wasn't like the other times. You cut me off every time I tried to ask her a question. You've never shut me out of a case before. I want you to tell me what's going on," he demanded.

"I told you. It's nothing."

Isaac shook his head. "I don't want to hear it. You're a good detective, Al, and I've learned a lot from you, but even a *rookie* like me can see you're dropping the ball with this one. That's not like you. Whether you like it or not, I'm your partner, and we work these cases together. Tell me what's going on."

Al looked at him for a long moment before diverting his eyes to the wall commemorating fallen officers. "Kimberly Hamilton," he finally said.

Just as Isaac suspected. "That was fifteen years ago. What does Tessa James have to do with that case?"

Al shrugged and looked out the window to the left of the squad room. "Who cares how long ago it was? It happened. It was a mistake I can never undo. She'd have been thirty-two this week. If I'd listened to her parents – to my gut – she might still be alive. Maybe she'd be married with a couple of kids. But I didn't listen to my gut. I thought she was a troubled kid who ran away. Because of me, the killer had time to murder her and get rid of the body."

Isaac's voice softened. "Al, you know you couldn't have prevented her murder. She never even made it to the movie. She was dead hours before she was even supposed to be home for curfew, before her parents even contacted you."

"I know." Al suddenly looked like somebody had let the air out of him. His hulking frame seemed to sag.

"That still doesn't explain what you have against Tessa James," Isaac prodded gently. His partner seemed to be on the verge of unraveling.

"Do you remember who Kimberly's killer was?"

Isaac shrugged. "It was one of her friends, wasn't it?"

"A friend she was meeting at the movies. The one who told her parents she never made it to the theater, to be precise."

"How long till you figured it out?" Isaac asked. He'd only been twelve years old when the murder happened.

"A while. Too long."

"I still don't know what this has to do with Tessa James," Isaac urged. He could tell there was something his partner didn't want to tell him.

Al walked to his desk and sat. Isaac followed him and settled into the cracked vinyl seat across from his partner.

"She didn't report what she saw immediately. She waited more than twelve hours. Why?"

Staying quiet, Isaac knew this was Al's way of thinking through the details of a tough case.

"I got to thinking. Maybe it was because *she* murdered a woman. Maybe she waited that long so she could stash the body somewhere."

"We still don't even have a body," Isaac reminded his partner. "There's no proof of a murder."

"There is that woman we found on the creek bed," Al countered.

Isaac frowned. "The James woman said the Jane Doe isn't who she saw that night."

"Yeah, she *said*. But maybe it was, and she's just trying to pull a fast one on us. Or maybe she just imagined the whole thing."

"Why would you say that? Has she given any hint that she didn't see what she claimed to see?"

"Other than the fact that she didn't even believe herself at first? No. But her family has a history of mental illness. That suicide call I asked you to look up was her mother. From what I learned going through that report, she'd been crackers most of her life." Al leaned back in his chair and crossed his arms over his barrel chest.

Isaac followed his partner's line of thinking. "And you

think Tessa James is sick just because her mother was? That she hallucinated the whole thing about the murder last week?"

Al rolled his eyes to the ceiling, as though he was studying the speckled tiles above him. "Possibly. The point is, I feel stuck, and I hate it."

Detective Dunn leaned his elbows on Al's desk. "So, what do you think happened?"

Al sighed and rubbed the back of his neck. "I wish I knew. It's possible she saw the guy who lives in that house carrying one of his wife's mannequins around and deluded herself into believing she'd seen a young woman who'd been murdered," he reasoned. "On the other hand, it is still a possibility that Tessa James really saw what she thought she did. Unfortunately, we have no evidence to back up that scenario."

"What about the break-ins? Do you think they never happened?"

Chewing the inside of his cheek while he weighed the possibilities, Al finally said, "It's possible she staged the home invasions. It's also possible that she sent herself the threatening emails to back up the story she created."

"And the woman who was shot in her house?"

Al heaved himself out of the chair and began pacing behind his desk. "She'd recently had a relationship with Tessa's ex-husband."

"Do you get the impression that she would off somebody like that?" Detective Dunn challenged. "I know I only met her for a few minutes, but she seemed pretty stable."

"My gut says no," Al admitted, "but we won't know until the ballistics report comes back. We've also got people going through the victim's phone for any clues about her relationship with Tessa."

The phone on Al's desk rang. Isaac watched the creases on his partner's forehead deepen as he listened. His mouth had formed a grim line. After making a few notes, Al hung up and slid his gun into the holster under his arm.

"Looks like my gut was wrong," Al muttered as he rushed from the squad room, leaving his partner behind.

61

CAREFULLY BALANCING THE chopsticks between her fingers, Tessa plucked another bite of General Tso's chicken from her plate and popped it into her mouth before she dropped it. She'd never really learned how to use chopsticks, and now looked longingly at the plate of food she doubted would ever make it from point A to point B without landing in her lap. On the few occasions she'd actually used them, she always thought a drop cloth would have been more appropriate than a napkin.

"You're getting better," Drew observed.

Tessa looked up, and as she did, the chopsticks crossed into an X and the chicken she'd so carefully picked up landed with a thud on the edge of her plate before rolling onto the table.

"Don't be so sure," she said, picking up the runaway food with her fingers and putting it in her mouth.

"You are. Don't you remember the first time you used chopsticks? You got so frustrated you ended up spearing your food with the end and ate that way. I felt like I was dining with a cave-woman."

Tessa laughed with more sincerity than she had all day. With Camille being shot and the police questioning her, the last thing she'd expected tonight was to have a good time. Drew seemed to be going out of his way to keep her occupied, even though he couldn't hide his concern about Camille.

A frown crept onto her face where a smile had been just seconds before.

"If it's bothering you that much, you can use a fork," Drew said, pointing to her plate with his chopsticks.

She tried to smile but could only manage a grimace.

"Sorry," Drew muttered. "I'm trying to keep your mind off what's going on. I guess I'm failing miserably, aren't I?"

She shook her head. "It's not your fault. I'm just so mad."

Drew rested his chopsticks against the edge of the plate and folded his hands under his chin. "You didn't do anything wrong, Tess. Camille is the one who was in your house. You weren't even home. I know your devil's advocate scenario says it's possible, but I know you. You couldn't have done this."

"I should have been there, though."

Reaching across the table and turning her chin to face him, Drew said, "You know what happened to Camille. If you'd been there, it would be you lying in the hospital bed."

She looked at him reluctantly, then said, "I know, but if I had been there, Camille never would have been shot. I wouldn't have shot her. To tell you the truth, I probably wouldn't have shot anybody no matter what. Even when I heard the recording of that scratching noise and thought somebody was in the house, I didn't get my gun. I grabbed your old baseball bat that somehow ended up with my things when I moved out."

"See what I mean? They can't convict someone who doesn't have it in them to harm another human being."

"I appreciate the encouragement, but I'm pretty sure they can do whatever they want," Tessa countered.

They sat in thoughtful silence. The fact that Drew couldn't say he was positive that Tessa had been at his house when Camille was shot was going to hurt Tessa, and they both knew it.

"I'm their prime suspect, you know," Tessa said, stabbing a piece of chicken with her chopstick.

Drew's hand stopped mid-air. "Did they actually say that?"

"Basically. How could I not be?" She bit the chicken off the end of the chopstick and chewed, then swallowed hard. It stuck in her throat.

"But they didn't arrest you. That's something," Drew said, a feeble attempt at finding a silver lining. "They have no proof you did anything wrong because you didn't. All you've done is try to get them focused on solving a murder they can't find evidence of."

Tessa raised a shoulder and let it drop. She stood up from the table, walked to the silverware drawer, and returned holding a fork.

Drew chuckled.

"I really should stick with what I know," she said, shoveling a forkful of rice into her mouth. "Making someone with absolutely no dexterity use chopsticks should be reserved as a form of punishment." She took another bite. "Maybe they'll make me use chopsticks in jail."

"Don't say things like that," Drew said quietly.

"Sorry," Tessa mumbled. "You know, when Camille came to see me that night, I could see why you liked her. I mean, it was really creepy the way she was just looking in the window at me, but once I started talking to her, she actually seemed very sweet. Vulnerable, almost. And she's obviously crazy about you. Besides, a person would have to be blind not to notice how beautiful she is," Tessa said, absently swirling her fork around on her plate.

"She was at your house? Why didn't you tell me that?" Drew's mouth hung open, revealing a half-chewed mouthful of sweet and sour chicken.

"She didn't come inside," Tessa said, unsure why she felt the need to defend a woman who'd scared her half to death earlier in the week.

He laid his chopsticks on his plate and shook his head. "What was she thinking?"

"She was thinking she loves you," Tessa said, self-consciously tugging at the waist of her jeans. They'd been getting snug sine Drew waltzed back into her life providing take-out every night for the past week.

Awkward tension floated between them until Tessa broke the silence. "I think I'm going to watch a little TV before bed." She stood and picked up her dishes, Drew following suit. As they did, the doorbell rang.

They exchanged looks of dread, then, Drew set his plate back on the table and walked toward the front door. It was amazing how quickly something as simple as the chime of a doorbell could turn into a bad omen.

Drew walked back into the kitchen with Detective Jefferson following close behind. The look on the detective's face perfectly communicated the reason he was there.

Tessa inhaled sharply and cut a nervous glance at Drew. "I'm afraid you'll have to come with me," the detective said.

Numbness began in her face and worked its way down

to her fingertips. "I didn't do anything," she protested in a shaky voice.

Fearing she'd drop the plate she was holding, she set it down quickly, causing her fork to bounce off the plate. Rice flew everywhere.

Like the pieces of my life, she thought.

"I'm placing you under arrest for the attempted murder of Camille Walker." The words might have been routine, but that didn't make them any less frightening.

Drew took a step forward. "Hold on a second – "

"That won't do either of you any good, Mr. James," Detective Jefferson said, his tone cool.

"What evidence could you possibly have for arresting me?" Tessa demanded.

"For starters, the victim was shot in your home. Also, we've got your fingerprints on the weapon and the gun was recently fired. Oh, and the ammo matched the bullet that hit her." He ticked the points off on his fingers. "Shall I go on?"

Tessa looked at Drew, panic etched on her face.

As she did, the detective pulled handcuffs from his belt and extended them toward Tessa. "Turn around."

"Is this really necessary?" Drew protested.

"Stay out of it, sir," Detective Jefferson warned.

As he snapped the handcuffs onto her wrists, his words seemed to come from a million miles away. "Tessa James, I'm placing you under arrest for the attempted murder of Camille Walker…"

The cold steel cuffs heavy on her wrists, she walked numbly outside as the scowling detective rattled off the rest of the Miranda warning.

62

TESSA TOOK A sip of the water Detective Dunn had placed in front of her. With a shaking hand, she set it back on the table and crossed her arms tightly around herself.

Detective Dunn gave her a reassuring smile. "We have to record this. I'm sure you understand."

She nodded and watched as he reached halfway across the table and pressed the record button. He smiled again then looked down at the file in front of him.

When she'd met Dunn this morning, Tessa had instinctively liked him. He had a comforting presence, even though Detective Jefferson hadn't let him talk.

"Can you start by telling me how you know the victim, Camille Walker?" he began.

"Until a few days ago, she was dating my ex-husband, but I don't actually know her," Tessa responded.

"Go on," Detective Dunn encouraged.

"That's all I know. I think they were together for about three months, but you'd really have to ask him."

"And how well do you know the victim, personally?"

Tessa narrowed her eyes at Detective Dunn. "As I've already told you, I don't know her. I met her once, for about five minutes. That was it."

He looked back at the file he was holding. "And what was the occasion of your meeting?"

Tessa sighed, loosening her grip around her waist. "She showed up at my house one night. I was reading a book, and when I looked up, I saw her watching me through the window. I went outside to tell her to leave, then went back into my house. She left after that."

"I see. Would you say you felt threatened?" the detective pressed.

Tessa arched an eyebrow. What was this guy getting at? "Not threatened, no. It was unnerving to see a face staring at me through the window, but I resolved the issue."

"What reason did she give for being there?"

"Drew had just broken up with her that morning, and she was under the impression that he and I were getting back together. I assured her that wasn't the case." Tessa lifted the glass to her lips and took another slow drink. Her throat was parched.

Detective Dunn leaned back and casually rested an arm on the table. "Did she say anything else?"

Tessa shook her head. Despite the fact that Camille had spied on her, Tessa was genuinely sorry about how things were turning out for her.

"Must have been scary, considering how on edge you've been lately," the detective urged.

"Of course," Tessa admitted, "but when I realized who it was, I was fine. I had bigger things to worry about, and I was more concerned about a killer hunting me down than a human

Barbie trying to take me out. Honestly, I was relieved it was her and not some psychopathic madman."

Detective Dunn chuckled softly. "Tell me about last night."

"There's nothing to tell," Tessa challenged. "I've been staying at my ex-husband's house since mine was broken into for the second time."

The young detective nodded. "From what I understand, he can't exactly corroborate your alibi."

Tessa exhaled deeply and slumped in her chair. She shook her head. "No, he can't. I was sleeping in the guest room. The last time we saw each other was around seven o'clock when I went to the door to get a pizza from the delivery guy. I took it to my room and watched some TV, then went to sleep."

The door creaked as Detective Jefferson pushed it open. "I'll take it from here, Detective," he said, his jaw clenched.

Detective Dunn forced a smile. "Just trying to take some of the burden off you."

Detective Jefferson ignored the remark and settled into the chair next to his partner, ready to begin his own line of questioning. "Would you please state, for the record, why you might have wanted to shoot Camille Walker?"

Tessa lurched forward in her seat. "I did *not* shoot her!" she protested.

Ignoring Tessa's objection, Detective Jefferson moved on. "Tell me about your college degree."

"What? Why does my degree matter?"

"What did you study, Ms. James?" the older detective pressed.

"English. That's how I got the job rewriting stories for the news station."

"What else did you study?" Detective Jefferson challenged.

Tessa sighed. "Computer science. Why?"

"You would have the knowledge to send yourself an untraceable email." Detective Jefferson leaned forward and narrowed his eyes at Tessa.

"What email?" Tessa asked, then bit her lip as the meaning of his question registered. "You think I sent myself the threatening email? First of all, you can check my official transcript. No class I took would have given me the ability to create an untraceable email account. Secondly, why would I do that?"

Exhaling heavily, Detective Jefferson replied, "To create a boogeyman you could bring to us, all the while distracting us from your true intentions."

"Which would be?" Tessa licked her lips. She needed more water.

"Killing Ms. Walker." The detective said it nonchalantly, as if hurling accusations at an innocent person was a completely normal occurrence.

"I didn't try to kill her!" Tessa cried. "How many times do I need to tell you that? I was nowhere near my house when Camille was shot. I have no reason to want her dead. I haven't even fired my gun in months."

Detective Jefferson snorted. "Your gun was used to shoot her, and she was inside your house. We also found a text message from you on her cell phone, asking her to come to your house last night. I'm afraid the evidence doesn't lie." He leaned back in his chair and crossed his arms over his barrel chest, as if there was nothing else he needed to say.

"Maybe evidence doesn't lie, but people do. Whoever is trying to make me look guilty is lying. Someone could have easily broken into my house and used my gun to shoot her," Tessa objected. "It wouldn't be the first time someone got in.

Besides, I don't even have Camille's phone number. There is no sent message from my phone to her."

The older detective tilted his head. "That's the one hiccup. We've determined the text came from a burner phone, which can be purchased anywhere. They're untraceable," he admitted. "While it's true that we can't prove you bought the phone, you also can't prove you didn't. I'm sure you can understand that."

Tessa ran her fingers through her disheveled hair and leaned forward, her eyes wide with fear. "I think you need to consider the possibility that the bullet that hit Camille was intended for me." She shivered. "Let's not forget, these things started happening *after* I witnessed a murder victim being carried through that house."

Tapping his chin with an index finger, Detective Jefferson said, "Interesting theory. The only problem is that the text message asking her to come over suggests that she was the intended victim, not you."

Tessa's shoulders drooped. "But why would somebody shoot her in my house?"

"Exactly my point, Ms. James. It only makes sense if *you* were the shooter."

63

MACHINES BUZZED AND beeped in Camille's hospital room, sounding a hundred miles away as she drifted in and out of sleep. She was on a rotation of pain killers, staggered, so she was always medicated. She felt better, but now she was constantly tired and could only stay awake a few minutes at a time.

It never occurred to her that the hospital staff had agreed to so much medication so she'd sleep most of the day.

The dreams were bad, too. She was somewhere she knew she wasn't supposed to be, a shadowy figure chasing her through the darkness. The last dream was about a distorted winged creature, half man, half bird. One dream, though, wasn't like the rest. Instead of being in the dark, she was surrounded by a golden light. A man walked toward her. Even though she couldn't see his face, she felt at peace there with him.

Her latest dose of medication had been about ten minutes ago, and Camille was being gently lulled to sleep by the rhythmic beeping of her heart monitor. She felt warm and happy, sure that the golden light of her happiest dreams was just moments away.

"Camille," a gentle voice said.

She smiled. The was the first time he'd spoken in her dream.

"Camille." The voice was closer this time, but still muffled.

"Camille," it said, sharper this time.

She turned her head toward the door. There, she saw a tall man surrounded by a golden glow. "This is such a nice dream," she said sleepily, allowing her eyes to droop shut.

"Camille, wake up," the voice demanded.

She forced her eyes open and blinked several times. Finally, as a faint smile touched her lips, she managed to whisper, "Drew."

He had come. She'd known he would and now he was here. She knew he still cared for her, and his presence at such an awful time proved it. Her smile broadened. "I knew you'd come."

"Camille, what happened?"

"I got shot," she slurred, trying to shake off the drowsiness.

"The police came to my house and arrested Tessa. They said you were shot at her house. What on earth were you doing there?"

Camille felt as if she'd been slapped. The voice wasn't tender anymore. It sounded angry.

Using all the energy she had, she said, "She asked me to come."

Drew took a step closer and shook his head vehemently. "Tessa swears she didn't, and they arrested her for attempted murder." He began pacing around the small room, anxiously rubbing the back of his neck.

"She tried to kill me? I should have known. I knew she

was crazy," Camille remarked with a snort. She turned her head away from Drew. He wasn't there out of concern for her. His only concern was for Tessa.

"Tessa wasn't even there. She was at my house, where she's been for days. At least she was until the police took her away," he growled.

"Maybe she sneaked out. Ever think of that?" Camille snapped. "All I know is that I got a text from her asking me to come over."

"How did she get your number?" Drew countered.

Camille shrugged her shoulders into the pillow. "Beats me. Maybe she got it from your phone when you weren't looking. Or maybe you gave it to her. Either way, you shouldn't be here yelling at me. I didn't do anything wrong. You should be yelling at her for doing this to me."

Drew stopped pacing and dropped into the chair at Camille's bedside. Even to her groggy eyes, he looked exhausted.

She stretched a weak hand toward him, waiting for him to return the gesture. Instead, he just looked at her blankly. There was no affection in his eyes, only fatigue and suspicion.

"Don't be mad at me," Camille whined. "I'm the victim here."

Taking a slow, deep breath, he said, "Unless you know she didn't do it and got her arrested for it anyway. In that case, she's a victim, too."

"How could you even believe that?" Camille protested. "When have I ever intentionally hurt someone else?"

"Never, since I've known you," Drew admitted, leaning back in the chair. "But there's always a first time," he added.

"I'm appalled," Camille said, placing her hand on her chest for emphasis. "Absolutely appalled that you would even think such a thing about me." A tear squeezed from the corner of her eye and trickled down her cheek. "She shot me, and I'm the one you're mad at? That's not fair."

Drew sat there a long minute, obviously considering what she'd said.

It's a perfectly reasonable explanation, she thought. She fought to keep the dejected expression on her face.

"That sounds possible," Drew said thoughtfully. "But you're forgetting one thing."

"What's that?"

"I know Tessa. I know she'd never do something like this. And I guess, since she's being held in jail, it's up to me to prove she didn't do it." He stood and walked quickly out of the room.

Moments later, a nurse came in. "Are you alright, Ms. Walker?" she asked, worry etched on her face.

"I'm fine," Camille grumbled. "Why?"

"We have a monitor at the nurse's station that tells us if your blood pressure or heart rate gets too low. Since you lost so much blood, we've been keeping a close eye on you. This was quite a rapid change," the nurse said, pointing to the monitor.

Camille glanced at the screen. No, that certainly wasn't low.

"I just had a bad dream, that's all," Camille said, willing herself to believe that her conversation with Drew had been just that. "I'm okay now."

Camille took a deep breath to relax as the nurse left the room. As she drifted off to sleep, the golden light surrounding the faceless man turned red. The feeling of peace was gone, replaced by the feeling of unshakable fear.

64

ISAAC DUNN WAS hot on Al's heels as he moved swiftly down the corridor back to the squad room. Isaac broke into a jog as Al turned right and headed straight for his desk.

Something was seriously wrong with his partner. In the two years he'd worked with Al, he'd never seen him as tense as he'd been since meeting Tessa James. Even when a suspect attacked him, he didn't get this rattled. He usually let even serious offenses roll off his back without so much as a twitch of his eye.

There had to be something else going on. It went deeper than his suspicion that Tessa might have made up a crime to report and then committed her own. From what Isaac could tell, nothing Tessa had said or done during the course of this investigation warranted such suspicion. Before, Isaac had chalked Al's attitude up to lingering guilt about the Kimberly Hamilton murder. That wasn't the case anymore.

He slowed his pace as he approached Al's desk. His eyes wandered to Al's hands. They were balled into fists and the veins were bulging in his wrists. The young detective's eyes darted around the large room that was filled with the sounds of ringing telephones, clicking keyboards, and the voices of coworkers. It all combined into a cacophony he feared would send his partner over the edge.

"Why don't we go somewhere a little quieter to talk?" Isaac suggested in a soothing voice.

"I don't want to talk," Al growled.

"I understand that, but I think it would be good for you to get some things off your chest," he urged.

Without a word, Al stood up from this chair and walked out of the squad room. "You coming?"

Taking long strides to keep up with his partner, Isaac fell into step beside him. They entered an empty interrogation room. Al paced around the room several times before taking a seat on the side of the table usually reserved for the suspect.

Isaac sat down across from him, careful to keep his body language casual. He crossed his right ankle over his left knee, leaned back in the chair, and rested an arm on the table between them. He said nothing, hoping Al would fill the silence. Instead, Al sat stoically, directing an icy stare in Isaac's direction.

"You feeling okay today, Al?"

"Yep. Never better," he snipped.

"Things okay with Darlene?"

"Peachy."

I've got to get him to stop stonewalling me, Isaac thought. Time to come at him from a different angle. He gathered his thoughts and said, "You know, sometimes when I'm working a case, it strikes a nerve and becomes personal. Sometimes the victim, a suspect, or even a witness reminds me of someone I know. Sometimes I like the person I'm reminded of, sometimes

I don't. In those cases, it's really hard to be objective. Ever feel like that?" Isaac paused, waiting expectantly.

Al leaned back in his chair and crossed his arms over his barrel chest. It wasn't the reaction Isaac had hoped for. He'd have to prod. "Does that sound like something that might be going on with you?"

Al snorted. "Don't waste your psychological tactics on me. I took that class, too. You thought if you shared something about yourself, I'd suddenly feel like spilling the beans about why I haven't been myself lately."

Isaac narrowed his eyes.

Al's body visibly relaxed a little. "Yes, I'm fully aware I'm on the verge of acting like a jerk."

Isaac smirked. "I'm afraid we're way past 'verge,' buddy." His tone became more serious. "Is there anything I can do?"

"Just keep alert," Al suggested. "The reality is, you never know who you're dealing with or what that person is capable of." With that, Al rose from his chair, walked past his partner, opened the door, and pulled it shut behind him.

"What's that supposed to mean?" Isaac muttered.

As he sat alone in the interrogation room trying to make sense of what was going on inside his partner's head, a scenario formed in his mind. If he was right, Al would never be able to be objective about this case.

Or any one like it.

65

THE FIRE CRACKLED as Harold Raymond stared into the flames dancing before him. Even though it was the middle of summer, he'd found that as he got older it was harder to stay warm. Sometimes, after a particularly stressful day at work, he'd light a fire and stare at it for hours, contemplating how a single choice could impact the way a person's whole life would turn out.

He'd considered that in his own life, and on the nights he couldn't leave the concern for his clients at the office, he'd considered it for their lives, too. It had been a long time since a client haunted him the way Tessa James did. It was those eyes. He was sure he'd seen them before. And something about her screamed danger. Not that he believed in any of that psychic mumbo-jumbo, but he'd sensed a darkness around her from the first time she walked into his office.

Here was a woman who'd done the best she could given what must have been a terrifying and lonely upbringing. She was functioning rather well in her daily life, even though she lacked any close and meaningful relationships. She didn't have the support system she desperately needed, but, even without those relationships, she'd managed to avoid the drama so many of his clients thrived on.

His last client of the week, an aging socialite who seemed to breed drama in her own life and the lives of anyone who came close to her, complained because a friend she considered socially beneath her hadn't invited her to a party. When he questioned her about why she cared whether or not she'd been invited to a party she thought would be dull anyway, she'd harrumphed and spent the rest of the session sulking.

It was next to impossible to stay focused on her endless complaining about the woes of high society when there were people like Tessa James out there who genuinely needed help and wanted to change.

The kitchen timer beeped, pulling him from his thoughts. His frozen lasagna was done. He rose from the recliner in front of the fireplace and walked slowly to the kitchen.

I'm getting too old for this, he thought. So much drama in so many lives. I didn't begin practicing for that. I did it so I could help people with legitimate problems overcome their obstacles and go on to lead fulfilling and productive lives. Not so I could play rent-a-friend to people who just want to belly-ache about problems they create in their own lives, then get angry any time I point out their own contribution to their troubles.

He grabbed a potholder from the drawer to the left of the oven, then withdrew the small foil pan and placed it on the plate he had waiting. Carrying it back to the living room, Harold settled back into his chair and decided it was time to cut back on his practice.

No exceptions this time.

Not even for someone like Tessa James, who'd sounded so desperate, almost like calling to make an appointment with him was her last resort. He was getting too old and too tired to keep it up.

He picked up the remote from the small table beside the chair and clicked on the TV. Even though the news rarely did anything but depress him, he felt it was important to stay informed on current events, no matter how horrible they were.

The ten o'clock news was just beginning, and he lamented that he was just now getting around to eating dinner. Cutting a fork-sized bite of lasagna from the pan, he lifted it to his mouth and blew on it. Just before he took a bite, the image on the TV screen stopped him cold. He replaced the fork, put the lasagna on the table and leaned forward, turning up the TV.

"...the woman found shot in a home on Highland Avenue has officially been identified as Camille Walker..." the reporter was saying.

Highland Avenue. A memory pricked Dr. Raymond's brain, and a bolt of electricity went through him. Tessa James lived on Highland Avenue. Hadn't she mentioned something about a woman by the name of Camille Walker at her last appointment? Something about her being in a relationship with Tessa's ex-husband and spying on Tessa through the window?

"...we have just confirmed that an arrest has been made. Tessa James was taken into custody earlier this evening..." the reporter continued.

Harold's head spun. Tessa James, arrested?

Suddenly glad he'd taken the time to write down his thoughts about her, he grabbed the briefcase containing his notes, stuffed his feet into his shoes, and dashed out the door, the fire still burning in the fireplace, his lasagna uneaten.

66

DREW RAN OUT of his house through the rain with the small overnight bag he'd packed for Tessa.

If they even let her have it, he mused.

This is all so unbelievable, he thought as he climbed into his car and slammed the door. Tossing the bag on the passenger seat, he put the key in the ignition and turned.

Nothing.

He tried again. Again, nothing happened. Not even a sputter.

Cursing under his breath, Drew got out, went back inside, and grabbed the keys to Tessa's car. After a silent prayer, he turned the key and breathed a sigh of relief when her car roared to life. He backed out of the driveway and made his way to the police station.

As he gripped the steering wheel tightly, he was herded from one red light to another.

"Whoever designed the traffic light system ensured that if you get stuck at one, you'll get stuck at all of them," he fumed. I don't have time wait through them. Tessa needs my help.

How could anyone believe Tessa would try to kill another human being? he wondered. The answer immediately came to mind. To everyone else, Tessa seemed distant, even cold, and when her temper flared, she could be downright mean. The reality was, though, that being cold and detached was her way of protecting herself against the people she was afraid of – which was everybody. But for that detective to believe Tessa had actually shot Camille was ridiculous.

You believe it a little bit, too, though, don't you? his subconscious whispered.

"No!" he shouted and banged the steering wheel with the palm of his hand. "Tessa doesn't have it in her to hurt someone else. She just doesn't."

A knot formed in Drew's stomach. He'd been shocked when he learned that Tessa had a gun, and she *had* been under a lot of strain lately. Was it possible that she was even more scared than she let on? What if she really had gone to her house and heard someone there, then just freaked out and shot?

Drew shook his head vigorously. *There's no way*. He knew Tessa. She had a cool head and wouldn't just go shooting blindly, even if she was scared.

But what if she wasn't shooting blindly? the small voice whispered again. Camille did get a text from Tessa asking her to come over.

Drew pounded the steering wheel again. "No! She wasn't even there. She was at home with me." He lowered his voice and whispered, "I need her to have been at home with me…"

67

IT BEGAN RAINING sometime while Harold Raymond was sitting in front of his fireplace considering the plight of his clients. Now, as he sat behind the steering wheel of his car, he squinted and leaned forward so he could see through the downpour. His wipers swished back and forth across the windshield as fast as they could, but they still didn't get the job done. With his failing eyesight, he usually tried to avoid driving in the dark, especially when it rained. He and his eye doctor had both agreed he could be a hazard to other drivers.

Tonight called for an exception.

He blinked in an attempt to make the yellow lights reflecting off the slick road go away, but he was out of luck. He never thought it was a big deal that he didn't live near the police station. In his sixty-plus years, he'd never needed to. Now he had to drive across town in the rain and darkness, praying he'd make it there in one piece.

Whatever it was about Tessa that had been bothering him since he first saw her was nagging at him again. What was it? Why did he keep thinking he knew her from somewhere?

Now, more than ever, he felt the pressure to remember. Doing everything he could to coax the memory from his brain, he still came up empty.

A horn blared. Tires squealed on the wet asphalt. Harold turned his steering wheel sharply to avoid sideswiping the car in the next lane.

"Well, it's not worth dying for," he muttered as he gripped the steering wheel tighter with both hands, heart beating with the intensity of a bass drum.

Realizing he was only halfway to his destination, he stared straight ahead and forced every other thought out of his mind. If he was going to help Tessa, he'd have to make it to the police station alive.

When he pulled into the parking lot, he felt as though a huge weight had been lifted from his chest. He gathered his jacket and briefcase from the passenger floorboard, covered his head, hugged the briefcase to his chest, then made a mad dash to the front doors.

I really hope plan A works, he thought as a tall man held the door open for him. But if not, maybe they'll consider my other one.

If they did, he'd have his work cut out for him convincing Tessa it was a good idea.

68

WHY DID I waive my right to an attorney? Tessa thought, anguished.

The reply entered her mind immediately: *Because I didn't do anything wrong and thought I could get them to understand that. That's why.*

She'd truly believed that once she presented her own defense to the detectives, they'd agree that she had nothing to do with Camille's shooting and let her go. Surely they'd see that just because she *could* have sneaked out of the house last night didn't mean she actually *did*. Any reasonable person would see that, right?

Except the detectives, who seemed to be waiting to pin this on her.

Tessa shook her head in disbelief and wondered what Mama would have had to say about all this.

Glancing around the room, Tessa noted there was no clock. Probably an attempt to disorient the suspect, she thought. In my case, it's working.

It seemed like forever since Detectives Jefferson and Dunn left, but there was no way to really know.

She looked longingly at the empty water glass sitting on the table. It had only been half full when they gave it to her, and she desperately wanted more.

It's just as well, she told herself. They probably wouldn't let me go to the bathroom, anyway.

Tessa turned toward the door at the sound of the knob rattling. She hoped for good news, but the look on Detective Dunn's face told her there wasn't any. She licked her dry lips and looked over his shoulder. "Where's Detective Jefferson?"

"He's working on something else," Detective Dunn replied, then lowered himself into the chair he'd occupied earlier.

As the detective silently observed her, Tessa shifted uncomfortably in her wobbly chair. She took a deep, shuddering breath, then asked, "Is it too late to ask for a lawyer?"

"No," he confirmed, then rose from his seat. "Do you have one in mind?"

Tessa bit her bottom lip and shook her head. Her hands, which had been only trembling, shook harder. "I'll need a public defender."

She tried to shake the hopelessness that settled over her. No one could protect her from what this nightmare threatened to bring.

69

DR. HAROLD RAYMOND nodded briefly at the man holding the door for him then walked toward the desk sergeant as fast as his aging legs could carry him. His mission was so absorbing his thoughts that he barely noticed that the man who'd held the door for him was following close behind.

When he reached the desk sergeant, he said urgently, "I need to talk to someone about a person who was arrested tonight."

"What's the name?" the desk sergeant droned. The name plate said the bored man's name was Sergeant Mitch Holland.

"I'm Dr. Harold Raymond."

Sergeant Holland looked up. "Not *your* name. What's the name of the person you want information about?"

The psychologist cleared his throat. "Oh. Yes, of course," he muttered. "Tessa James."

"I want to talk to someone about her, too," said the voice behind him.

Dr. Raymond looked away from the officer in front of him to notice the man who'd held the door for him was the same one speaking. He'd taken a step forward and was now standing beside him.

"And who might you be?" the sergeant asked.

"Andrew James. Tessa's ex-husband."

He looked at Dr. Raymond. "And you?"

"As I already mentioned, my name is Dr. Harold Raymond."

"A doctor?"

"A psychologist, actually," Harold clarified.

The officer raised his eyebrows.

Without acknowledging the man's curiosity, Dr. Raymond thrust his jaw forward. "I would like to speak with the arresting officer, please," he said, then, tapping the desk with a slender index finger, added, "Right now."

Sergeant Holland pointed to a row of chairs lined against the wall opposite his desk. "Please sit there. I'll let the detective know you'd like to speak to him."

Dr. Raymond did as instructed and settled into a hard plastic chair.

"You, too," Sergeant Holland said to Drew.

"So, you're her psychologist?" Drew asked, following Dr. Raymond and taking the seat next to him.

Dr. Raymond's mouth drooped. "I'm afraid I cannot confirm nor deny that."

Drew nodded his understanding, then extended his hand. "I'm Andrew James."

"I'm sure this would be a pleasure under different circumstances," Dr. Raymond said, returning the handshake.

"How did you know Tessa was here?" Drew asked.

The older man leaned forward and clasped his hands together. "I saw on the news tonight that she had been arrested."

Drew rubbed the five-o'clock shadow on his face. "She was at my house when they arrested her." He leaned back in his chair and stretched his long legs out in front of him. "She didn't do it, you know. She wouldn't hurt anybody."

"I know," Dr. Raymond said softly.

"Any idea if she has legal counsel?" Drew asked hopefully.

The psychologist shook his head. "I know less than you do."

"You don't have to answer me, but I'm going to ask anyway. Do you think, from a psychological standpoint, that Tessa is capable of what they've accused her of?"

Dr. Raymond carefully considered how to answer. He was strict in his professional ethics and wouldn't budge when it came to client confidentiality. "It's hard to say what someone is capable of. Put in a certain situation, any one of us is capable of acting out of character. However…" He didn't go on, but the expression of doubt on his face spoke volumes.

Smiling sadly, Drew said, "I don't think so, either."

Clearing his throat, Dr. Raymond said, "So, you're Tessa's ex-husband?"

"Yeah, her *ex*-husband," Drew said, a sour note in his voice. "Not because I wanted to be done with her. Quite the opposite, actually. I just couldn't keep living with her constantly pushing me away."

"I see."

"I guess all I ended up doing was pushing *her* away and reinforcing the notion that she really couldn't trust me." Drew stood and began pacing around the chairs, the noises in the background grinding on his already frayed nerves. Finally, he reclaimed his seat and looked at Dr. Raymond, who appeared to be lost in thought. "I dated the victim, you know. That's part of the reason they suspect Tessa. I guess, in a way, this is all my fault."

Feigning surprise, Dr. Raymond widened his eyes. "I imagine this must be a difficult time for you. One woman you care about lying in a hospital bed, the other arrested for her attempted murder."

Drew grunted. "Camille – that's her name – was nice enough, and she liked to have a good time, but she's not my type. I could never really talk to her. But Tess… I've always been able to talk to her. All I ever wanted was for her to trust me, and now look what I've done." He leaned his head back against the wall and closed his eyes. "You're too easy to talk to," he said wryly.

The pain on this man's face made Dr. Raymond question whether or not, in this dire situation, he should loosen up on his ethics. Perhaps it wouldn't hurt to give the man a little hope. "No," he said finally. "I don't think Tessa is capable of hurting anyone. In fact, that's why I'm here. I sensed something was wrong last time I talked to her, so I began compiling my notes and observations so I could present them as evidence, if needed. I often serve as an expert witness during trials, so this is right up my alley, I'm afraid."

"Thank you for that. Tessa's had a rough go of it. Her mother was really, really sick. There was a time at the beginning of our marriage when her mom wouldn't even let me in her house. She thought I was coming to steal her thoughts. I assured her I have plenty of my own and had no need for hers, and in time, she eventually loosened up. It really wore Tessa out, but when her mom died, Tessa was devastated. It just took the spunk out of her for a while. It was like she didn't know what to do with herself without looking after her mom. She just, I don't know, changed somehow."

Dr. Raymond nodded in agreement. "Tessa is a resilient woman. She'll be okay," he assured Drew, then noticed him stiffen when a barrel-chested man in a suit approached them.

"Detective Jefferson," Drew said, standing. His voice was laced with tension. The detective didn't acknowledge him.

"Dr. Raymond. Nice to see you again. What can I do for you?" he queried. The detective's voice was pleasant when he spoke to the psychologist.

"I need to speak with you about Tessa James," he said, standing to meet the detective, who dwarfed him with his overall bulk.

The corners of Detective Jefferson's mouth dropped at the mention of Tessa's name, a reaction that wasn't lost on either of the men.

Looks like I've got my work cut out for me, he thought. Good thing I like a challenge. "Is there someplace we can go and talk?" It came out as more of a suggestion than a question.

Jerking his head toward the hall leading to the interrogation rooms, Detective Jefferson lead the way. Dr. Raymond followed, shooting a backward glance at Drew.

This wouldn't be an easy sell, but, unfortunately, it looked like it was necessary.

70

LOIS SIMMONS HUGGED her over-sized shoulder bag to her ample chest as she ducked her head and walked quickly down the hall away from the interview room and toward the door of the police station. Never in her wildest dreams would she have imagined she'd be giving her statement to a police detective after stumbling upon a shooting victim!

That poor woman, Lois thought. What was she doing getting herself shot in someone else's house? And right next door, too!

At least that nice Detective Jefferson had been kind enough to let me come in tonight, instead of insisting that I come right away. I had orders to fill, and I needed to get my bearings after what I found!

He wasn't nearly as grumpy as he'd looked when he left Tessa's house the other evening, and he'd been so understanding when I told him I had orders that couldn't wait. He didn't know cranky Mrs. Oliver, but he'd saved my hide by letting me complete her order. The nerve of that woman, demanding so much from me. I've only got two hands! Lois huffed, shaking her head. Some people just have no manners.

Like my next-door neighbor, apparently. To think she just shot that lady and left her to die. What kind of person would do something like that? Lois wondered, a chill racing up her spine at the idea that she'd been living next to a would-be killer for the past year. Who knows what else she's done?

"And to think I was so worried about not getting her my pound cake," Lois muttered, indignant that she'd put herself through so much just to make that lady a homemade treat. She shook her head.

"I guess you just never know about some people," she muttered as she approached the police station door.

Just as she was about to push it open, she stepped quickly to the side to avoid running into an older gentleman. A younger man was hot on his heels.

Lois spun to watch him walk away as his face registered in her mind.

She gasped. "That's the man who's been visiting Tessa all week!" He's so handsome, she admitted to herself, though she was disappointed in the kind of company he was keeping. I hope he didn't have anything to do with that poor young woman being shot.

Her mind settling on her beautiful but reserved neighbor, she reminded herself how easy it is to be deceived by a pretty face.

71

JACOB ARMISTEAD STARED at the ceiling fan whirring above his bed. Though it was almost completely dark, he'd been awake so long that his eyes had adjusted, and he could make out the outlines of his bedroom furniture.

His plans were unraveling. Or they would be if he'd had a plan to begin with.

He hadn't been able to get Tessa James out of his mind all week. Why had she chosen that night and that street, of all the streets in the city, to take a walk?

He'd been careless. He knew that. He'd taken advantage of the fact that he lived at the end of a quiet dead-end street in a house that was mostly hidden from view. That, coupled with his assumption that no one would be out on a stormy night, had caused him to slip. If he had just dragged the body instead of carrying it, he never would have been seen.

For the past six days, he'd felt like he was being hunted every waking moment. Each time he turned around, he expected that grumpy detective to be standing there, dangling handcuffs in his face.

It would have been easy to take care of the problem, but if anything happened to her after she reported what she'd seen, they'd nab him for sure.

Then, to make matters worse, Samantha had surprised him by getting home this evening instead of tomorrow morning. He needed those extra ten hours.

A grim smile tugged at his lips. Things might end up working out okay, after all.

He'd been watching Tessa that night when the other woman came to visit. He didn't think either of the women had seen him, but he needed to be sure. Both of them would have to be taken care of.

That was when he'd had the inspired idea to use a more roundabout way to get rid of the James woman, and also make sure the other one couldn't talk about the strange man lurking around. Thanks to his cousin, it hadn't been hard to get the other lady's cell phone number. Now Tessa James was in jail for shooting Camille Walker and the focus had been taken off him. The plan had been just about perfect, except for one thing.

The Walker lady didn't die.

Though unlikely, it was possible that she'd be able to identify him if she ever recovered.

Now he lay motionless, sweat saturating his pajamas. With shaking hands, he wiped the beads of sweat accumulating on his forehead. He assured himself he'd worn gloves and left no traces of his presence in that house. It wasn't his first time cleaning up after himself, and he was becoming increasingly certain it wouldn't be his last.

The covers rustled beside him and Samantha slipped her hand onto his chest. The dampness of his pajamas roused her from her sleep. "Are you okay, J?" she asked groggily.

"I'm fine," he said as he sat up and swung his feet over the edge of the bed. "It's just a little fever. All these loose ends must be compromising my immune system."

Samantha didn't hear his explanation. She was already snoring.

As he got up to splash some cold water on his face, he decided that Camille Walker was another loose end he would have to take care of.

Then he'd worry about the James woman.

72

TESSA'S HEART POUNDED as she sat in the waiting area of the admitting office late Sunday night. While she appreciated Dr. Raymond's willingness to go to bat for her, she didn't want to believe a seventy-two-hour stay at the state psychiatric hospital was all he'd been able to work out.

In the interrogation room at the police station, she'd thought anything would be better than a jail cell. Now, surrounded by other people waiting to be admitted, she thought a cell would be a better – and safer – option.

To her left was a visibly agitated young man who looked about twenty years old. His leg bounced up and down while he picked at his hand. He didn't raise his head or look at anyone. Tessa's initial impression was that he was so tightly wound that he could snap at any moment. He was accompanied by a man whose bulk rivaled that of an NFL football player.

At her right was a petite young woman who seemed to shrink right into the hard plastic chair. She, too, kept her eyes averted from everyone. She was alone, probably admitting herself voluntarily.

Several of the other chairs were occupied by people who looked like they were in the same position she was – waiting to be locked up, away from the rest of society, as a last resort. The difference was, they all had the blank stare of anticipation. Unlike Tessa, this probably wasn't their first stay at a psych hospital.

One by one, they were each called into a small room off the side of the waiting area. Soon, she was the only one left.

"Tessa James," an impersonal voice called from the direction of the room.

Her palms grew sweaty. What's going to happen back there? she wondered as her throat constricted. She looked at Detective Jefferson, who'd insisted he accompany her. He nodded slightly but didn't return her glance.

Standing slowly, she made her way to the unknown room, avoiding eye contact with hospital personnel. This is so humiliating, she thought. Is this how Mama felt when I had her admitted?

The attendant, a broad, unsmiling woman in navy blue scrubs, pointed to the examination table in the center of the room. "Sit," she commanded. There were no introductions, only instructions.

Tessa did as she was told, stifling the urge to tell the woman she didn't belong there. She was certain it wouldn't be the first time the woman heard that.

A man who'd been sitting quietly in the corner tossed her a hospital gown, told her to put it on, and left the room. The woman in scrubs scooted a privacy screen between her and Tessa and waited.

"Exactly what kind of exam am I having?" Tessa asked, her mouth suddenly dry. She didn't need more humiliation right now.

"A skin check," the female attendant said coolly without any inclination toward small talk.

"Skin check?" Tessa asked, the cool gown grasped in her clammy hands.

"We'll check for any wounds, abrasions, tattoos, or skin abnormalities. If we find any we'll take a picture and put it in your chart. That way we know what kind of condition you were in when you got here."

They'd be taking pictures of her? Tessa looked to her left to see a camera and ruler sitting on a table. She looked at the ceiling and took a deep, steadying breath. I can handle this, she reassured herself.

"I'm ready," Tessa said when she'd tied the last pair of strings together behind her back. The draft reminded her that she could kiss all efforts at modesty goodbye.

The woman moved the privacy screen and picked up the ruler. She knocked on the inside of the door, indicating for the man to come back in. He picked up the camera, and inch by inch they examined Tessa's body for anything unusual.

After what seemed like an hour, she was allowed to get dressed and instructed to go back to the waiting room to complete the admitting process. Detective Jefferson was right where she'd left him, his thumbs moving quickly on the screen of his phone.

"Thank you for waiting with me," Tessa said. Though his demeanor toward her had grown cold, this would be scarier if she was alone.

A nod was the detective's only response.

"I'm nervous," she admitted.

He shrugged one shoulder and looked at her only long enough to say, "I'm sure you'll be fine."

Before her lips could form the words she hoped would illicit a more comforting response, the man behind the desk across the room called her name.

Before she got up, she lowered her trembling voice and looked toward Detective Jefferson, who still wouldn't make eye contact, and said, "What you think isn't true. I didn't shoot Camille," then walked to the attendant who'd called her.

Willing herself to stay calm, she reminded herself this wasn't the place to unravel. Not if she wanted to be sure she got out of here when the seventy-two hours was up.

She divulged the deepest, darkest secrets of her mental history to someone not nearly as comforting as Dr. Raymond. The guy asking the questions was huge. Everybody who worked there was big. The men could have been bouncers, the women at least the size of an average man.

After filling out the last line of the admitting form, two people who had been standing in the doorway were waved over. They stepped forward and motioned for her to go with them. Smiling warmly, the woman said, "This way."

Tessa looked back at Detective Jefferson just long enough to notice that he didn't give so much as a glance in her direction.

With a quick reminder to herself that she could handle whatever happened these next three days, she disappeared through the door and into what she was certain would be one of the darkest hours of her life.

73

AFTER DROPPING HIS keys on the small table in the entryway of his house, Drew walked slowly to the kitchen and grabbed a beer from the refrigerator. The plates from dinner remained on the kitchen counter, bearing witness to his hurried exit.

He removed the cap from the bottle and took a long gulp. The day had been a long one. He almost couldn't believe it was just this afternoon that Tessa had come to his office to tell him Camille had been shot. When she told him the police suspected her, he'd almost laughed, but the distress on her face told him it hadn't been a joke. It seemed like days had passed since then.

Unsure what else to do, Drew grabbed the keys to Tessa's car and drove to her house. Nobody would be there, but he hoped it would give him some answers. As he parked at the curb in front of her rented bungalow, he saw that the yellow police tape was still stretched across the front door, a testament to the night before. The door was closed and the windows were dark. The crime scene investigators had probably come and gone, collecting whatever evidence they needed to figure out who shot Camille, or it seemed increasingly likely, whatever evidence they could find that pointed to Tessa.

He stayed in the car, images from the past week bombarding his mind. The two of them laughing over enchiladas, Tessa falling asleep during the movie and her near meltdown when she found him in the shower the next morning.

A sad smile began to form on his lips.

They were good together. Even when they were fighting, something still worked.

What if they convict her for this? What kind of life will she have? What kind of life will I have? Drew wondered.

Turning the key in the ignition, he pulled away from the curb and started back toward his house.

It was half past midnight, too late to really do anything to help Tessa. First thing in the morning, he vowed, I'll start looking into what really happened.

74

THE FIRE HAD reduced to glowing embers by the time Harold Raymond got home from the police station. Still untouched, the lasagna had become an unappetizing, congealed mess.

He shook his head at the way the day had turned out. As with any other day, it began with promise. He tried to approach each day as though it had endless wonderful possibilities. Ever the optimist, he could usually extract even the slightest glimmer of light from a day that otherwise seemed hopeless.

Not today, though.

Try as he might, he couldn't come up with a single good thing. Sure, he'd had the foresight to compile a psychological defense for Tessa, but even now he wondered if his interference had been in her best interest.

His goal had been to present solid psychological evidence that Tessa James, while at times appearing cold and distant, was not psychologically capable of taking the life of another human being. But Judge Gavin Cooper, before whom he'd appeared in court numerous times as an expert witness, didn't want to hear it. He just said Tessa hadn't been in treatment long enough for him to have a firm judgment on what she was or wasn't capable of.

That was when he tried plan B.

It seemed like a good idea at the time, and Judge Cooper was more than willing to hear him out when he suggested she be placed under inpatient psychiatric care due to a rapid increase in stress. Now he wasn't so sure it was a good idea.

He'd been allowed to speak with her briefly before they took her, and the panic on her face when they told her the judge agreed to let her be held at a psychiatric facility sent a wave of regret over him. He'd known what she was thinking.

Just like Mama.

As he scraped the cold lasagna into the trash can, he became troubled as he remembered something he'd noticed while speaking to the judge. Detective Jefferson had also been present, making his case about why Tessa should remain in custody at the detention center. Out of the corner of his eye, Dr. Raymond had seen Detective Jefferson sternly and almost imperceptibly shake his head when he'd asked for Tessa to go free until they were able to get a court date.

Judge Cooper was paying more attention to the detective's reaction than to what I was saying, Harold remembered. But when I moved on to my request that she be moved to the state psychiatric hospital instead of jail, it seemed that Detective Jefferson almost had a look of pleasure. At the detective's cue, Judge Cooper had readily agreed to that alternative.

As Harold flipped off the kitchen light and walked through the living room and down the hall to his bedroom, he made a mental note to pay more attention to Detective Jefferson and the judge. It didn't sit right with him. He couldn't help but wonder why a judge would base his legal decisions on the wishes of a police detective.

75

IT WAS WELL past midnight when Tessa reached the unit she'd be calling home for the next three days. It was mostly dark; the only light in the unit was the centrally located nurse's station. Four hallways branched off from there like spokes in a wheel. Each of the four halls were dark, lit dimly with security lights and the eerie glow of the exit sign at the far end of each one.

This unit looked similar to the one Tessa's mom had been on, even though it was a different hospital. She'd only visited once though, having been asked not to return. After she'd left, Tessa's mom had gotten so agitated that she'd been impossible to handle for days.

Poor Mama, Tessa thought. You must have been so scared. I know I am.

"The women's bedrooms are down this hall, the men's down this one. The common area and dining room are down this hall, and the medication room is back there," Jessie, the female nurse who'd picked her up from the admitting office said, pointing in each direction as she spoke. "The women's bathroom is right here next to the nurse's station," she said, pointing around the corner. "There are sheets and a blanket already on the bed, and we have toiletry items and a community clothing room if you need anything."

"Thank you," Tessa said, following the nurse down the women's hallway. They stopped at the second bedroom on the left.

"Here you are," Jessie said. "You can take the bed under the window. Your roommate is Martha. She's a really quiet old lady and sleeps like a log. You likely won't hear from her until breakfast."

Good, Tessa thought as she crossed the sparse room to a bed that bore a striking resemblance to an army cot. The sheets were tucked tightly around the thin mattress. It creaked as she sat down. "Jessie?" Tessa said, just as the nurse was turning to leave.

"Yeah?"

"What does this band mean?" she asked, holding her arm out.

"When each patient is admitted, they get a red band, meaning you're under close observation by hospital staff and have to stay on the unit at all times," the young nurse explained. "After being assessed by your psychiatrist, he'll decide whether or not to upgrade you to a yellow band. That means you can go off the unit, with supervision, to the dining room or one of the recovery classes we offer. If you do well with that, you could be upgraded to a green band, which means you can be trusted to go off the unit by yourself, without supervision. Try to think of them as traffic lights: stop, proceed with caution, and go. Let's just hope you're not here long enough to earn the green one." Jessie smiled and left the room.

Tessa kicked off her shoes and lay down on the bed, tucking her hands behind her head. She rolled to her side, hoping the next few days wouldn't be as horrible as she imagined.

The strain of the day had taken its toll on her, and Tessa eventually drifted off to sleep – only to be jolted awake by yelling. It sounded distant, but it was definitely coming from somewhere down the hall. Mingled with the angry voices was the sound of driving rain pounding against the security-screened window above her bed. The heavy metal door securing the unit opened and slammed shut, followed by the sound of a dozen feet pounding on the hard tile floor. A primal scream rose above the noise, sounding like that of a cornered animal.

Muffled orders came from one of the men, followed by the sound of a squeaky bed. Over and over the sound echoed off the walls and floor, like someone was bucking in the bed.

Tessa's stomach rolled. She didn't know much about psychiatric hospitals, but there was no doubt one of the patients had become violent and was placed in restraints. A tear slipped from the corner of her eye as she turned toward the wall and curled up into a ball, a vain attempt to shield herself from whatever was happening just a few halls over.

A jagged bolt of lightning flashed in the sky outside the window, briefly illuminating the room's meager furnishings. Her roommate was barely a bump under the threadbare blanket.

The commotion hadn't disturbed her.

Tessa jumped as thunder cracked so loudly she felt the vibrations deep in her chest. Another tear slipped down her cheek and soaked into the pillow.

Seventy-two hours. She was stuck here with no hope of getting out for three days. In three days, she'd either be going home or going to jail.

She squeezed her eyes closed and pulled the blanket up, securing it under her chin. After what seemed like hours, she finally drifted off to the cadence of Martha's snoring.

Somehow, she'd find a way to survive the darkest hour of her life.

76

FRUSTRATED, DREW SNAPPED off the radio and settled back into the driver's seat of Tessa's car. The news didn't have anything new to report about Camille's shooting or Tessa's arrest, and nobody had bothered to call him with an update. He still hadn't called AAA to get the battery replaced in his own car, and, considering what he was up against, he didn't want to wait around for hours for them to show up at his door.

He'd barely slept last night, replaying everything that happened yesterday. He nervously tapped the steering wheel with the tips of his fingers and looked at the clock. He'd only been sitting in the parking lot outside Dr. Raymond's office for ten minutes, but it felt like it had been five times that long.

Oh, Camille, Drew thought. Why were you at Tessa's house? What did you hope to gain from going there?

A wave of guilt followed his relief that Camille had taken the bullet instead of Tessa. Nobody deserves that, he reminded himself, then shuddered at the possibility that whoever shot Camille had done it by mistake. If the intended target was Tessa, what would stop him from trying again?

A movement in Drew's peripheral caught his attention. A middle-aged woman he assumed was the receptionist darted from her car to the front door and quickly unlocked it, disappearing through a door to her right.

Again, Drew glanced at the clock: 8:03. She was three minutes late, and Dr. Raymond had yet to show up.

Deciding to take a chance with the receptionist, he dashed across the parking lot hoping to have a chance to speak with Dr. Raymond as soon as he got to work. The bell on the glass door jingled as he jerked it open.

Startled, the receptionist eyed him suspiciously and asked, "Can I help you?"

"I need to speak with Dr. Raymond right away," he demanded.

Worry flitted across the woman's face.

"It's about one of his patients," he added, realizing that this wasn't the place to behave like a raving lunatic. "If he isn't here yet, do you have a number where I can reach him?"

"I'm sorry, sir," the receptionist said, taking a step back. "I can't give out his personal number. If you would like to have a seat and wait for him, you may. You must understand, however, that his clients come first, and you are not to interfere with their treatment."

Realizing it was useless to press, Drew turned to sit in the upholstered chair closest to the door. She reminds me of Dorothy, he thought.

Drew picked up a magazine and mindlessly flipped through it, then tossed it aside. Nothing on the planet could distract him. He bounced his leg up and down, eyes darting around the room. He briefly met the receptionist's gaze, only to realize that she wasn't just suspicious of his behavior – there was fear in her eyes.

Should I tell her why I'm here? he wondered. Surely she has a right to know why I'm acting like the poster child for untreated adult ADHD.

Just as he opened his mouth, the bells on the door jingled again as Dr. Raymond entered, already apologizing for his tardiness. The receptionist shot her eyes toward Drew and mouthed something to Dr. Raymond. He gave her a comforting nod and said, "It's okay."

Drew stood as the psychologist approached him.

"I understand you need to speak to me," the older man said, a knowing expression on his face.

"Yes. Do you have a few minutes?"

"Of course. Come with me."

Drew followed Dr. Raymond into his office and took the seat offered to him. He imagined Tessa sitting here, telling Dr. Raymond things she'd never told anyone else.

"What can I do for you?" Dr. Raymond asked, depositing his briefcase on his desk, then circling around to sit in the chair opposite Drew.

Fighting back a stab of jealously about Tessa opening up to a total stranger, Drew said, "It's about Tessa."

Dr. Raymond nodded. "I assumed as much, yes."

"Well, there's something that's been bothering me." Drew paused then said, "Two things, actually."

"Go on," Dr. Raymond encouraged.

"What is going to happen to her at that place? She absolutely does *not* belong in a psych hospital. Also, what on earth was Camille doing at Tessa's house? I just can't believe Tessa would ask her to come over."

Dr. Raymond narrowed his eyes. "And you think I have the answer to that?"

"I couldn't sleep last night, so I did some research on you. Apparently, you're very good at reading people. Knowing when they're lying... stuff like that. So good, in fact, that the state often calls you as an expert witness during murder trials. There are quite a few articles that mention you."

Dr. Raymond crossed his legs at the ankles and scratched his jaw line. "That's true, but I don't see what that has to do with Tessa's predicament. What exactly do you want from me?"

Drew paused, weighing his words. He might only have one shot at getting Dr. Raymond to help him, and he didn't want to blow it. "I want your professional opinion about what might be going on here," Drew said, then added, "Of course I would pay you your typical hourly rate."

The psychologist continued to rub his chin. "I see. And where do you propose I begin?"

Drew thrust his jaw forward and met Dr. Raymond's questioning eyes with his own steely determination. "First, we go to the hospital and find out why Camille is lying about Tessa asking her to meet." Drew took a deep breath. "Then, find out if Tessa was actually the intended target."

77

TESSA WOKE MONDAY morning with a splitting headache as light illuminated the wire-covered window above her bed. She figured it was well after six thirty, given how bright it was outside.

"Good morning, Ms. James," a young woman with red hair and purple scrubs said as she knocked softly on the door.

Jessie had told Tessa last night that breakfast would be served in the small dining room off the common area at seven-thirty.

Despite the headache, Tessa's stomach growled. She hadn't eaten since dinner last night, and even then, she hadn't eaten much.

She sat up, rubbed her temples, and slipped her feet back into her shoes. Wobbling slightly as she stood, she braced herself against the sorry excuse for a bed until she regained her equilibrium. Then she quietly followed the nurse down the hallway, past the nurse's station, past a small room where a man slept on a bed, wrist and ankle restraints dangling off the side, and down another hall until she was standing in what she assumed was the common area. Several tables and chairs were on the side of the room, and a sofa, love seat, and two chairs – all made of what appeared to be dense foam – were positioned in front of a TV that was bolted to the wall. Even though the room was ugly and depressing, she took comfort in knowing all the furniture could be disinfected.

"My name is Ann," said the pretty young nurse. "Breakfast is in there." She pointed toward a small room with tables and chairs. "Please let me know if you need anything."

"Thank you," Tessa said as Ann turned and walked back down the hall toward the bedrooms.

As she stood there, several patients shuffled past her to the dining room. None of them made eye contact or even looked her way. Her stomach growled again, and she followed them into the dining room, where a man in scrubs was distributing breakfast trays.

Breakfast in hand, Tessa claimed a seat at the table in the farthest corner of the room, as far as she could get from the other patients. She grimaced at the meal in front of her: scrambled eggs that looked as though they'd been powder a few hours ago and a piece of toast that could double as a paper weight. The canned fruit cocktail and a small container of orange juice were the only semi-redeeming things on the plate. She downed both of them in about a minute, thinking this was just the place to lose the weight she'd put on in the past week.

"Thank you," she muttered as she returned the tray to the young man and walked from the room.

I guess it's time to see about those toiletries, she thought ruefully, wishing they'd have let her keep the overnight bag Drew had brought to the police station. Tessa decided her clothes from yesterday didn't smell bad enough to send her running to the communal clothing closet just yet.

Armed with a towel and washcloth as thick as tissue paper, a small bottle of shampoo that smelled like disinfectant, and a bar of soap the size of her thumbnail, she made her way to the bathroom. There was no line for the shower, and, judging by the smell emanating from some of the rooms, she wasn't surprised.

After hurrying through a shower, she dressed and went back to her room, where she found Martha sitting on the edge of her bed, fiddling with her bun. To Tessa, she looked like the quintessential grandmother. It saddened her that a woman of her age would be stuck in a place like this instead of surrounded by her children and grandchildren.

Tessa dropped the shampoo bottle on her bed and turned to her roommate. "Hi. I'm Tessa."

Martha watched her for a moment, then said, "It's best I don't get to know you. That bed has more turnover than a motel room rented by the hour."

Tessa furrowed her brows. "What do you mean?"

"Most people don't stay long. How long are you in for?"

The corner of Tessa's mouth drooped at her roommate's use of prison lingo. "Seventy-two hours."

"See?"

Tessa sat on her bed. "How long have you been here?"

"Three months," Martha replied with a shrug.

"Three months! Whatever for?" She seemed perfectly lucid to Tessa.

"Stabbing my husband," Martha said, nonchalantly. "They told me they ran out of room on the geriatric unit, so they stuck me up here with the wackos. No offense. I'm here until a bed opens up there, which usually means somebody has to die or the family decides take care of their kooky old relatives."

So much for being the quintessential grandmother, Tessa thought and busied herself making the bed. I'll have to keep my eye on this one.

"Please forgive me if I don't seem to remember you next time I see you. They think I have dementia," Martha said, then leaned forward and whispered, "and I let them think what they want."

Tessa smiled at the old woman. Husband-stabber or not, she liked Martha. "It'll be our little secret."

After making her bed, she headed to the common room. There was no remote for the TV, so she pressed the button under the screen to turn it on.

From somewhere behind her, someone shouted, "Hey! Keep it down!" She turned to see the angry-looking young man from the admitting office sitting in the back corner of the room, mostly covered by a ratty old blanket.

"Sorry," Tessa mumbled. She'd have to keep an eye on him, too. Her gut told her the list of people to watch around here would keep growing.

Giving up on the TV, Tessa walked to the nurse's station. "Is there a book lying around that I could borrow?"

Ann looked up from the form she was filling out. "Not on the unit, but I can run down to the library and get something if you'd like," she offered.

"That would be great. Something by Hemingway or Fitzgerald, if they have it."

Ann cocked an eyebrow. "I can't promise we have anything like that, but I'll try." Nodding to the vicinity behind Tessa, Ann said, "It looks like your psychiatrist wants to see you."

Tessa turned her head at the sound of someone approaching. As the man got closer, a bolt of lightning went through Tessa's midsection.

A look of recognition registered on the psychiatrist's face, then disappeared as quickly as it had come. He extended his hand toward her and introduced himself. "I'm Dr. Jacob Armistead. I'll be treating you for the duration of your stay."

78

DREW PRESSED THE button to call the elevator that would take him to Camille's hospital room. She probably wouldn't be happy to see him again after he walked out on her yesterday, but he hoped she'd at least be willing to talk to Dr. Raymond.

He'd just have to spin it the right way.

Dr. Raymond's secretary had called Drew just as he was pulling into the hospital parking lot. She said Dr. Raymond was running late, but he'd be on his way as soon as he wrapped things up with his client. Meredith, the secretary, had warmed up considerably after Dr. Raymond assured her everything was okay, and that Drew was consulting him about a criminal case someone he knew was involved in. Tessa's name was never mentioned, though Drew was almost certain Meredith had heard about it on the news.

It's amazing how people act differently when they're not afraid, he mused, then immediately thought of Tessa. She must be terrified. The one time she went to visit her mother at the hospital, she'd come home shaky, telling Drew she didn't feel safe. He'd always known that Tessa's biggest fear was that one day she'd end up like her mom.

That fear could only be magnified right now.

The elevator doors opened, and the sterile smell of hospital disinfectant hit him like a wall. He hated this place, and he hated why he was here.

Camille had been moved from the ICU, so he didn't have to announce his presence at the nurse's station anymore. For that, he was glad. He didn't need some nosy nurse coming in to see how they were doing in case things got heated.

As he walked down the hall, he noticed a nurse coming out of Camille's room. He slowed his pace so they didn't cross paths and waited until she was gone before gently tapping on the door.

"Come in," Camille said, sounding stronger than she had yesterday.

"Hi," he said, still standing by the door.

A smile brightened Camille's face. "It's good to see you," she said softly.

He nodded.

"To what do I owe this pleasure?" she asked.

He narrowed his eyes, never taking his gaze from her face. "We need to talk about something."

She winced as she sat up in bed. "What is it, Drew?" A cloud of worry darkened her pretty face.

From behind him, Drew heard someone clear their throat. He turned to see Dr. Raymond standing in the doorway.

Camille looked from Drew to Dr. Raymond and back to Drew. "Who's this?"

Dr. Raymond stepped forward. "My name is Harold Raymond. I'm a psychologist. Drew is an acquaintance of mine, and he told me what happened. He was concerned that you might have been traumatized and asked me to talk to you." Dr. Raymond hesitated then said, "He's very worried about this whole situation."

This guy is good, Drew thought. At least part of that was true. He was very worried about the effect this situation would have – on Tessa.

Camille reached a hand toward Drew and a smile once again spread across her face. "That is so sweet of you."

Drew flicked his eyes toward Dr. Raymond, who didn't return the look. Only a twitch of his eye indicated any reaction.

"May I speak with you for a few minutes?" Dr. Raymond asked gently. "Alone?"

As Drew took a step toward the door, Camille protested. "Drew can stay."

Shaking his head firmly, Dr. Raymond said, "It would really be better if he wasn't here for this. Sometimes it's hard to let our loved ones see us at our most vulnerable. We want to be strong in front of them and end up hiding our emotions. You have to take care of yourself, Camille, and let yourself express the feelings you've been keeping inside since that terrible moment." He paused for emphasis. "That's when real healing can begin."

Camille sighed dramatically. "Oh, perhaps you're right. I *have* been trying to be too strong. I wouldn't want Drew to see me so upset."

She wiggled her fingers at Drew as he turned to leave.

Balling his hands into fists, he wondered if Dr. Raymond would be able to get anything useful out of her.

He glanced at his watch. He was paying Dr. Raymond for a full hour. With time to kill, he went to the waiting room, grabbed a snack from the vending machine, then rode the elevator down to the hospital lobby and walked outside, where the summer sunshine was lost on him.

He sat on a bench in front of the hospital entrance and pulled his cell phone from his pocket. After popping the top of his soda can, he took a long swig, then looked up the information for the psych hospital. He punched the number into his phone and waited.

An impersonal voice answered, and a pit formed in Drew's stomach as he realized the lady's chilliness was probably what Tessa was surrounded by. "Please hold," she said, then before Drew had a chance to respond, she clicked off.

Drew took a long drink of Dr. Pepper, forcing it to go down over the lump in his throat.

"I'm sorry," the woman said when she came back on the line. "I can't confirm or deny that we have a patient by that name here."

Drew frowned. She didn't sound sorry. "I know she's there," Drew insisted, "and it's very important that I speak with her."

"Sir, I've already told you. I can't confirm or deny the presence of a patient by that name at this hospital. I'm afraid I can't help you."

There was a click, and then a dial tone.

Drew involuntarily squeezed the can, causing the sticky liquid to spill out over his hand. How could he possibly make sure Tessa was safe if they wouldn't even admit she was there?

Drew hoped Dr. Raymond was having better luck than he was. At this rate, it would be a miracle if anything could help Tessa.

79

TESSA SIGHED AS she watched the other patients mill around the bottom floor of the hospital, going from one recovery class to the next. Thanks to her newly acquired yellow wrist band, she was scheduled to attend anger management class in fifteen minutes – if she could find the energy to get off the bench she was occupying. Staring blankly at the tile floor in front of her, the pattern changed from one image to another as her eyes shifted focus. A lion, an old man, a lizard, a demon. She shook her head to clear the images from her mind. Her brain felt so foggy.

This morning, just after breakfast, they'd given her some kind of medication. The nurse said it would help relax and balance her. That was just before she'd met her psychiatrist, Dr. Armistead.

Tessa had refused the medication at first. She didn't need a pill to relax her; she needed to get out of there. But the nurse told her that cooperation would help her chances of getting discharged. After that, she'd taken whatever was offered, especially if it would "relax" her. And now, here she was, stuck in a hospital with a killer for a doctor, so drugged so she wouldn't even have the energy to defend herself.

Maybe that was the point.

The instinct to protect herself kept her from mentioning the reaction she was having to the medication. Telling someone she'd been purposely put in a drug-induced stupor wouldn't help her case, either.

What did they give me?

The bell rang, alerting her it was time for her next scheduled class. With all the energy she could muster, she stood from the bench and walked slowly down the hall toward room 156. Anger management. She walked in and plopped down in the closest chair she could find.

The instructor walked to the front and began rambling about anger being a natural response to threat, then Tessa tuned her out. She wasn't angry. She wasn't even mildly irritated. She was drugged. The medication wasn't balancing her; it was tipping her mental capacity toward oblivion. Her eyes stung. She felt powerless to stop what was happening to her. It had all started with one horrible night and snowballed from there.

And now, here she was, locked in a psychiatric hospital for three days under the care of a monster, completely at his mercy.

Despite the medication, her heart began to hammer. I know he recognized me. I saw it on his face. But there's nothing I can do, she thought, dangerously close to despair.

For the next forty minutes, she drifted in and out of her fog. Then the bell rang, telling everyone it was time to go back to their units. Tessa shuffled as quickly as her body would carry her in an effort to keep up with the rest of the patients from her unit, then followed the nursing assistant up to her home away from home.

As soon as the door opened, Tessa scanned the unit for Ann. She was a nurse, so maybe she'd be able to tell Tessa what she'd taken that had knocked her sideways. Catching Ann's eye behind the nurse's station, Tessa motioned that she needed to speak with her.

"Can you tell me what kind of medication they gave me this morning?" Tessa asked quietly.

Ann held up one finger and went back behind the desk. She pulled out a chart and flipped through it. She closed it and pointed in the direction of the common room. "Come with me," she instructed, then started down the hall.

Tessa trudged down the long hallway and settled into a chair in the far corner. "Something is wrong," she explained. "Since I took that medication, I've been in a fog. My body feels like it weighs a thousand pounds. I feel like I'm walking through water. I have no appetite. This isn't me."

Ann nodded. "Haldol makes most people tired. Some people get hit harder than others, and it looks like you're one of them. Honestly, I have no idea why you're on that medication. Your chart says you're in here because of an increase in stress, but Haldol is an anti-psychotic."

Tessa snorted. "Stress? Is that what it says? I've been the victim of two home invasions in the past week and was arrested for the attempted murder of my ex-husband's girlfriend. Not to mention the fact that I saw someone carrying a dead body." She clenched her jaw, anger replacing some of her drowsiness. "So, yeah. I guess you could say I've been stressed."

Ann's eyes widened as she leaned away from Tessa. "Did you do it?"

Tessa shook her head. "No, I didn't," she said emphatically. "But I am in trouble. Clearly."

Should she tell Ann about Dr. Armistead, or would calling her psychiatrist a murderer only sink her chances of surviving this place?

Tessa's intuition kicked in, and she decided to take a chance. "Do patients ever go missing from here? I mean, just sort of disappear?"

Ann nodded. "Margo," she said quietly.

"Margo?"

Ann cleared her throat and quickly glanced around the room. Lowering her voice to a whisper, she said, "Margo Lang was a patient for several months. She was brilliant, but very paranoid." A small smile touched Ann's lips. "She'd sometimes quote Chaucer to me. Such a zest for life, despite her illness. Toward the end of her time here, she began to make accusations against some of the male staff. We all wrote it off as the ranting of an unstable woman, but, about a week ago, she just disappeared. Her doctor didn't discharge her, and no one saw her leave the unit. She was good at slipping in and out, though. Sometimes she'd be missing for a day or two at a time, then just show back up. That's what we all figured happened this time." She paused and swallowed hard. "But it's been a week, and my gut tells me she isn't coming back. Why do you ask?"

Tessa shook her head but said nothing. It made sense. A psychiatrist would be able to do a lot of things to a patient without anyone ever finding out. After all, who would believe a psych patient instead of a doctor?

"So, what do I do?" Tessa asked. "I can't take that stuff again. My mind just can't think straight."

Leaning to within inches of Tessa's face, Ann looked deep into her eyes and whispered, "Cheek your meds."

Tessa blinked. "What?"

"Cheek your meds. Don't swallow them. Hold them in your cheek until you can spit them out. I'll see what I can do to make sure you're not given that stuff again."

"Won't you get in trouble for telling me to do that?"

"Only if anyone finds out. Just make sure you keep quiet about it," Ann warned.

Several patients walked into the common room, muttering to themselves.

Ann stood and quickly walked from the room, with only a backward glance to give any indication she'd spoken with Tessa.

Feeling a bit more energized, Tessa stood and walked back to her room. If her gut was right, Margo Lang was the woman she'd seen last Monday night, and her psychiatrist was the one who killed her. She needed to find a way to let someone know what she'd found, then get herself out of this place.

80

AFTER THE LATE night escorting Tessa James to the psychiatric hospital, Al Jefferson made an executive decision to go in to work late. Not that anybody would mind. He knew he'd been a real jerk lately.

He poured coffee into his jumbo-sized travel mug and grabbed a cinnamon roll from the plastic package. Leaning over the sink, he took a bite. A little stale, he thought ruefully, then took another bite. Darlene would be all over him about his cholesterol if she saw what he was eating. Fortunately, she was visiting her mom out of town. Without her there to nag him about his health, he relished eating the way he had before she moved in. As annoying as her nagging was, though, the woman could cook. To his disappointment, even the cinnamon roll didn't taste as good as it would have before he met her.

He quickly took a sip of hot coffee, almost taking the skin off the roof of his mouth in the process.

I guess that lousy cinnamon roll is the last thing I'll be able to taste for a while, he thought as he grabbed his keys and headed out the door.

Another day of crime and criminals too dumb to get away with anything awaited him.

The drive to the station was pleasant. Rush hour traffic ended hours ago. No one cut him off or refused to let him merge into another lane. Most mornings he wanted to pull people over just for being rude.

With his caseload lighter than it had been in years, his main concern was the alleged murder victim Tessa James had brought to his attention, the attempted murder of Camille Walker, and the girl in the creek bed. As far as he was concerned, two of those cases were pretty much wrapped up. Tessa would go to jail for shooting the Walker lady, and with no evidence for what she'd claimed to witness, there wasn't much of a case to investigate.

Al had been so preoccupied with Tessa James, that he'd forgotten to check in with Isaac about any developments with the girl by the creek bed.

Crossing the squad room, he avoided eye contact with anyone who glanced in his direction until he passed Isaac's desk. Not even looking at his partner, Al hooked a finger and said, "My desk. We need to talk."

Isaac dutifully followed him. He sat down, crossed his ankles, and folded his hands. Al thought he looked suspiciously like someone who'd just been sent to the principal's office.

"What's up, Al?" Detective Dunn asked.

Al placed his travel mug on his desk and dropped into his chair with such force it sounded like the wheels were going to break off their casters. "What's going on with the Jane Doe they found by the creek bed?"

Isaac uncrossed his ankles and shifted in his seat. He

cleared his throat and said, "Well, we have an identity, so technically she's not a Jane Doe anymore."

Al spread his hands in front of himself. "Is this not something you thought you should mention?"

"Identity was just established last night, when you'd insisted on being the one to escort Tessa James to the psychiatric hospital even though a uniformed officer could have easily done it," Isaac spat. "Then you decided to come to work four hours late today and not tell anybody, not to mention the fact that you haven't been answering your phone."

Ignoring the remark, Al pressed, "Well? Who is she?"

Isaac held up a finger and went back to his own desk. He came back carrying a folder, then reclaimed his seat and crossed his ankle over his knee, spreading the file the length of his tibia. He shuffled some papers, then said, "Let's see. She's been identified as Amanda Meyers. Twenty-three years old, born and raised in Boston. Moved here five years ago for college, then just stuck around after that."

The young detective shuffled more papers. "It looks like she's been unemployed for the past year. Apparently she was let go from her job at a local marketing firm for strange behavior. Her temper had gotten bad and they worried she was going to snap. She was fired, the firm citing that she created a hostile working environment. After that, nobody saw much of her, but she was still able to make her rent. We think maybe her parents were paying for her apartment. Anyway, a couple months ago, she made a scene at a restaurant and became violent. She was arrested. After a psychological evaluation, she was found to have bipolar disorder and was admitted to the state psychiatric hospital."

At Al's questioning look, Isaac said, "I was here most of the night digging up information on her."

"She was a psych patient that ended up dead? When was she discharged from the hospital?"

"No idea. I'm about to head over there. Wanna come?" Isaac offered.

Al grunted. "Just try and stop me."

81

DREW PRESSED HIS foot against the accelerator, weaving in and out of traffic, trying to get to the hospital as quickly as he could.

It was after the lunch rush, so traffic had cleared considerably. Still, he felt like he'd never make it there.

Nearly twenty minutes later, he parked, and hurried from his car, only to see that Detective Jefferson had parked close to the building and was walking toward the hospital entrance.

From a distance, Drew watched the detective enter the hospital, pausing only briefly at the front desk to flash his badge, then breezing past the receptionist. As Drew ascended the hospital steps, he saw Detective Jefferson disappearing down a long hall.

Breathing heavily, Drew pointed in the detective's direction and huffed, "I need to get in there."

"Are you also with the police?" the receptionist asked, shuffling the papers on her desk. It was clear she didn't care about Drew's urgency or his collapsing lungs.

"I need to catch up with the detective you just let in," he said, deliberately slowing his breathing.

"I'm sorry, sir. If you aren't with the detectives, you can't come in. Visiting hours don't resume until six o'clock this evening. You'll have to come back then." She shoved the stack of papers into a folder and finally made eye contact. "Perhaps you should tell your detective friend to wait for you next time," she suggested.

Six o'clock? He glanced at his watch. That was still four hours away. His mind reeled at what could happen to Tessa during that time. His gut clenched. Here she was, a sane, adult woman being locked away and denied the basic right of seeing friends and family. And for what?

Because someone had framed Tessa for shooting Camille.

Drew slammed his fist on the desk and turned to walk away. The receptionist flinched.

"I'll be back at exactly six o'clock," he muttered and walked back out into the humid summer air.

This is ridiculous, he thought angrily. I can't even imagine what this is doing to Tessa. She's really going to have a hard time trusting people when this is all over.

He shook his head and walked slowly back to his car, disgusted with his own inability to help her. He slid behind the wheel of his car and stared absently at the neglected building.

Dr. Raymond would be finished with Camille by now. Backing out of his parking spot, he drove back in the same direction from which he'd come. To kill time between now and visiting hours, Drew would find out what Dr. Raymond had to say about Camille.

If they could somehow prove Tessa hadn't been the one

to send Camille that text message, the judge might lift the seventy-two-hour hold so Tessa could go home.

But how could he possibly prove that?

She wasn't going to be released, and unless a miracle happened, things would only get worse for her.

82

KNOCKING BRISKLY ON Dr. Jacob Armistead's office door, Detectives Jefferson and Dunn walked in without permission and claimed chairs on the opposite side of the doctor's desk.

"Detective Jefferson. It's a pleasure to see you again," the psychiatrist said through a tight smile, looking back and forth between the two detectives.

"Likewise," Al clipped. "So, Doc, how's it going around here? Your patients doing okay?"

The doctor nodded. "They're doing very well. Progress is being made."

"Swell."

"Okay, then," Detective Isaac Dunn interrupted. "Let's get started. I'm sure the good doctor is very busy."

"I am," Dr. Armistead agreed, "but please, ask me anything."

The corners of Al's mouth twitched, then formed a smile. "Tell us about Amanda Meyers."

"Who?" The psychiatrist narrowed his eyes and shook his

head, but the beads of sweat on his upper lip and forehead betrayed his anxiety.

"Amanda Meyers," Detective Jefferson repeated. "She was a patient here until about three days ago, give or take."

Dr. Armistead looked up at the ceiling as if willing recognition to drop from the sky. "Amanda Meyers. Amanda Meyers," he repeated. "I'm trying to remember, but the name just doesn't ring a bell."

"Try harder," Detective Dunn said in a sharp tone that was uncharacteristic of his typical easygoing manner.

"I'm sorry. I have no recollection of a patient by that name. Let me send for a nurse. They spend more time with the patients than we do." He picked up the phone and pressed a single button. "Can you please come to my office right away?" he said when someone answered.

"It should only be a minute," he said, replacing the phone on its cradle.

This guy is full of it, Al thought as he studied the faint cracks on the wall. He knows exactly who we're talking about.

A young woman with red hair and purple scrubs knocked, then pushed the door open. "You needed to see me?"

Dr. Armistead waved a hand in her direction. "Detectives, this is Ann Mason. She's one of the nurses on my unit. Ann, these are Detectives Jefferson and Dunn. They need to know if you remember a patient named Amanda Meyers."

"Sure," Ann said. "She wasn't on our unit, but she was in one of the recovery classes I teach about medication management."

"Ann is in school to become a nurse practitioner. Her knowledge about medication is much more extensive and useful than that of our other nurses," the doctor explained, admiration lilting his voice.

"When did you last see her?" Isaac asked.

Ann knitted her eyebrows as she thought. "Four days ago, I think. She seemed really distracted in class, almost like she was worried about something. After class, I asked her if she was okay, and she said she was. That was the last time I saw or spoke to her." Ann's face clouded. "Why?"

"I'm afraid she's passed away," Al said, watching the nurse's reaction carefully.

Ann placed a hand on her chest. "That's awful. How did she die?"

"I'm afraid we're not at liberty to discuss that at this time," Isaac responded. "It's an ongoing investigation. I'm sure you understand."

"Of course," Ann said, nodding softly. "Such a shame. She really was a nice girl. Bright, too. She could have had a great life ahead of her once she got back on her feet."

On a hunch, Al said, "Do you know if she was taking her medication regularly? I know she wasn't on your unit, but, since you taught her medication class, maybe you'd know."

Ann flicked her eyes toward the psychiatrist, then nodded vigorously. "Oh, yes. She was doing extremely well. She was lucid, outgoing, friendly. She hadn't had a manic episode in weeks. I think her doctor was planning to discharge her soon."

Isaac retrieved the small notepad from his pocket. "And who might that be?"

"Dr. Wilma Robinson on unit 3C. You should talk to her. She and Amanda had a really good rapport."

"Thank you, Ann. That will be all," Dr. Armistead said, dismissing her.

Nodding slightly at Detectives Jefferson and Dunn, she turned and left the room.

"I told you a nurse would be more helpful than I. Now, if you'll excuse me, I have several patients to speak with this afternoon."

"Of course," the detectives said in unison as they rose from their chairs. "And I know you'll be willing to speak with us again if we have more questions," Al added.

The detectives left the room before the doctor could respond.

After quickly asking a janitor how to get to unit 3C, they found Dr. Wilma Robinson in her office. An attractive fiftyish woman with short ash blond hair and intelligent green eyes, she was a stark contrast to the ferret-like Jacob Armistead who, despite his arrogance, always seemed like he was sweating.

After a quick introduction, Isaac said, "We understand you had a patient named Amanda Meyers."

Dr. Robinson narrowed her eyes and said, "I'm afraid I cannot discuss patients – "

"She's dead," Al interrupted, "so that rule no longer applies."

"Dead?" Dr. Robinson gasped. "How can she be dead?"

"When did you last see her?" Isaac asked, using the gentle tone he saved for friends and family of victims.

"About three days ago," Dr. Robinson said, eyes searching her desk for something that obviously wasn't there. "I met with her in the morning to discuss her treatment plan and the next steps she would have to take to be discharged, but by that afternoon, she'd just... disappeared."

"What do you mean 'disappeared'?" Al asked.

"We thought she'd just taken off, escaped somehow. Amanda was doing extremely well and was frustrated that I hadn't discharged her yet. She wasn't entirely pleased with what

I had to say in our meeting. I thought she took matters into her own hands." Dr. Robinson's eyes watered. "What happened to her?"

"I'm afraid we can't discuss that," Isaac said in a soothing voice, "but we're wondering if anything happened here lately. Something that might have given her a reason to feel like she had to leave?"

Dr. Robinson tapped her chin with an index finger as she thought, then, as if a light bulb had switched on in her head, she snapped her fingers. "There was one thing. At first, I thought it was because she might be slipping into a manic episode. That's why I held off discharging her. Sometimes, during one of her episodes, she'd make wild accusations about people, so, I'm ashamed to say, we didn't take her concern seriously. But she was taking her meds and had been doing so well, and I began to wonder if there might be something to it."

Al tightened his face to mask his impatience. "Go on."

"She said she saw someone who works here harassing another patient. Amanda was adamant that it happened. We looked into all the employees on our unit but came up with nothing. When I told her that, she became furious. She reminded me that not everyone worked on our unit. That's when she told me who it was. I wanted to believe her, but I couldn't bring myself to admit that what she was saying could be true. I mean, he's such a good doctor. And she's such a caring and compassionate nurse…"

"Who did Ms. Meyers accuse, Dr. Robinson?" Detective Dunn urged.

The doctor hesitated, then sighed. "Dr. Jacob Armistead, on unit 3B and his number one nurse, Ann."

The two detectives exchanged glances. "What was the name of the patient Ms. Meyers said they were harassing?"

"Margo Lang."

"Thank you for your time. You've been incredibly helpful," Al said as he and Detective Dunn walked quickly out of the office, retracing their path out of the hospital.

Checking on Tessa would have to wait.

The pieces were falling into place, and the case against Jacob Armistead was coming together. Now it seemed as though he had an accomplice.

"What now?" Isaac asked once they were outside. The creases in Isaac's forehead deepened as he studied his partner.

"I need to get Tessa James out of there," he said, holding his phone to his ear. "No matter what unit she's on, she's at the mercy of that monster."

83

JACOB ARMISTEAD QUICKLY shut the door behind Detectives Jefferson and Dunn. As he paced around his small office, beads of sweat popped up on the back of his neck. Soon there were dark circles under his arms. He continued to pace, the walls closing in on him.

How stupid could I have been?

I shouldn't have let Amanda Meyers off this property, he berated himself. Now they suspect that I was responsible for her death.

Plagued by the weight of a lifetime in jail, he sat heavily into his chair and put his head in his hands, flexing his clammy fingers in his hair.

Ann would talk, he knew she would. She'd do whatever she had to do to make sure she didn't end up in jail. She was young, with a bright future ahead of her. They'd give her a plea bargain for sure.

Side by side on his desk were a picture of his mother as a young woman and one of him and Samantha, smiling broadly, with the Pacific Ocean behind them. Their honeymoon to

Hawaii had been one of the happiest times of his life. For the first time, someone had accepted him unconditionally. She didn't care that he wasn't the most handsome man in the room; she was just fascinated by his brain.

So much like his mother.

It looked like the one weakness he'd allowed himself was finally going to be his undoing. It was exhilarating to have control over beautiful women. He'd done it many times, relishing the thrill every time they were helpless against him.

Now Ann would betray him, and she'd force him to teach her a lesson, too.

He made a fist with his bony hand and slammed it down on the desk until it hurt. Tears streamed down his cheeks.

Real men don't cry! he mentally shouted at himself, but try as he might, he couldn't curb the flow. His mother's words kept echoing in his brain. *Real men don't cry!*

A knock at the door stopped the tears he'd been unable to control.

"Dr. Armistead?" a voice called from the other side of the door.

"Yes?" he replied, the word coming out as a croak. He cleared his throat and repeated, "Yes?"

"Remember that you have several patients to see before the end of the day."

"Yes. Thank you."

He took a few minutes to compose himself, then quickly ran through the patient schedule. His eyes stopped on the last one on the list: Tessa James. Another beautiful woman who'd hurtled him into a tailspin. If she'd kept her nose in her own business, none of this would have happened.

Squelching his growing anger, he pushed back his chair

and stood. With his back straight from renewed determination, he took a short glance in the small mirror on the wall and crossed the room to the door. With a deep breath he pulled it open and stepped from his office, determined to take care of the problem once and for all.

Even if it cost him everything.

84

SITTING IN THE common room, Tessa couldn't decide whether to laugh or cry. Three other patients circled the room, each one talking to what she assumed were the voices in their heads. On their own they weren't making sense, but together they sounded like a chorus of insanity. A tear threatened to slip from the corner of her eye as she laughed at the absurdity of the situation.

She was trapped here with the person she was certain had been behind the home invasions, the threatening email, and Camille's attempted murder – not to mention the murder that started this whole mess. If she could somehow make it through two more days, she'd get to leave, either for jail or to go back to her normal life.

But these people. For them, this was their normal life, and it pained Tessa to think about the bleakness of their futures. She'd seen it in Mama, but somehow this was different. Mama had her, and Tessa had done her best to keep her out of places like this. For the most part, she'd been successful.

Who is watching out for these people? she wondered. Do

they have families that are understanding and compassionate, doing their best to make sure their loved ones get the highest quality treatment they can afford? Or do they bury their skeletons away in securely locked closets, hiding them from the rest of the world?

Another tear slipped from her eye. She wasn't being fair. The families weren't to blame. Tessa understood very well how difficult it was to live with someone who was sick enough to be in the hospital. Everybody was just trying to do their best with a terrible situation.

At a sound behind her, she turned her head slightly to see Dr. Armistead leaning against the doorway of the common room. Slouching down in her chair so he wouldn't see her, she pretended to be interested in the show on TV while still keeping a watchful eye on her doctor. The truth was, she didn't care about the rerun of the only crime drama that seemed to occupy daytime television. A quick glance around the room told her no one else cared either.

Except one person. Her psychiatrist was standing there, watching it with the same intensity of a student studying for a final exam.

85

DREW PLOPPED INTO a chair in the waiting room while Meredith announced his presence to Dr. Raymond.

Trying to ignore the annoyance in her voice, he wondered how upset Dr. Raymond would be that he'd left him at the hospital with no warning. He seems like a reasonable man, Drew thought. I'm sure he'll understand why I had to go.

Looking up at the sound of Dr. Raymond's office door opening, Drew noted that he didn't look upset. He breathed a sigh of relief. He needed this man's help and couldn't afford to upset him.

Dr. Raymond escorted the client he'd been seeing to the door, gave him a few words of encouragement, then turned to Drew. "You look haggard," he observed. He motioned for Drew to follow him into his office, where he bent over to retrieve a bottle of water from the mini fridge he kept under his desk and held it out to Drew.

Accepting the water, Drew twisted the cap off the bottle and took a long drink, then massaged the lines in his forehead.

He noted that the creases were deeper than they had been just this morning.

"This whole thing is just so unfair. Tessa has spent her whole life thinking the worst about people, and now it seems like the entire human race is out to prove her right."

"Meaning?" Dr. Raymond settled into the wingback chair across from Drew and arched a thick eyebrow.

Drew shrugged. "I went to the hospital to see her. When I was there, I saw Detective Jefferson in the parking lot. It looked like he was in a hurry, like something was wrong. I tried to catch up with him, but when I finally got into the hospital he was gone, and they wouldn't let me visit Tessa. Said I had to come back at six o'clock if I wanted to see her." Drew leaned forward and rubbed the stubble on his face. "I just have a bad feeling that she's in trouble and there's not a thing I can do to stop it."

The psychologist stood and crossed the room to his desk. He picked up the phone, and as he dialed, he turned to Drew and said, "I'll check in on Tessa." He waited as the phone rang, then said, "Yes. This is Dr. Harold Raymond. A client of mine is currently being treated there, and I believe it would be beneficial for me to come by and check on her."

Drew waited as Dr. Raymond listened. He found himself growing more impatient with each passing moment.

"Wonderful!" Dr. Raymond said. "I'm on my way." He replaced the receiver and turned to Drew. "Coming?"

Springing to his feet, Drew crossed the room in a few long strides and walked out of the office as Dr. Raymond held the door for him. He stopped and looked into the older man's eyes. "Thanks for helping me."

Dr. Raymond shook his head. "I'm not doing it for you. When I agree to take on a new client, I'm making a commitment to do everything I can to ensure he or she gets the best possible treatment. If my recommendation to have her held at the hospital instead of jail could place her at an increased risk, it's my responsibility to make it right."

"Tessa made the right decision when she started coming to see you," Drew said. This man was truly going above and beyond what would normally be expected of him.

A flush of pink crept up Dr. Raymond's neck. "Thank you."

Drew swallowed the lump in his throat and followed Dr. Raymond to the parking lot, surprised that a man of his age and stature could move so fast.

"You follow me in your car," he called to Drew as he veered to the right and stopped at a black Mercedes. "I'll wait for you in the lobby to make sure they let you in."

Drew nodded and quickly climbed into his own car, encouraged that, with Dr. Raymond's help, Tessa might have a fighting chance.

Dr. Raymond peeled out of the parking lot with Drew on his tail. For the next twenty minutes, Drew struggled to keep up with the aging psychologist, who was weaving in and out of rush hour traffic, handling his luxury sedan as if he were in the Daytona 500.

Relieved to finally be sitting still in the hospital parking lot, Drew took only a moment to regain his composure after the high-octane drive across town.

Apparently, Dr. Raymond needed no time – he was soon sprinting up the steps in front of the hospital. Drew followed suit and dashed across the parking lot to catch him, silently praying that they could stop the situation from getting worse.

86

AT FIVE O'CLOCK med pass, Tessa stood with the rest of the patients in line, waiting for the nurse to hand them their medication. When she was at the front of the line, she accepted a small cup that looked like something you'd put ketchup in at a fast-food joint, brought it to her lips, then tossed her head back. Quickly using her tongue to stuff the pill deep into her cheek, she took a drink of water from the cup the nurse offered, careful not to let the water touch the pill.

She left the medication room and walked quickly to the bathroom, where she spit the semi-dissolved pill into the toilet. The bitter residue clung to her tongue. Tessa flushed the pill, took a big drink from the sink faucet, and swished. Another drink helped erase the aftertaste completely.

Dinner would be served in a half hour. With most of the effects from her morning dose worn off, Tessa looked forward to eating. Her breakfast had been a meager bowl of fruit cocktail and a small container of orange juice. Lunch consisted of a ham sandwich with a pickle spear and French fries that looked like they'd been sitting under a heat lamp for days.

She hadn't even touched it.

Settling into the common room with most of the other patients, she again pretended to be interested in what was on TV. Her stomach growled. That's a good sign, she thought.

As she waited, two male nursing assistants walked up to her. "Tessa, please come with us," one said in a gruff, baritone voice.

Her mouth suddenly dry, she looked from one unsmiling face to the other, back and forth, searching them for some clue about what was going on. "Where are you taking me?" she asked. Two large men coming to take her away was a page torn right out of Mama's worst nightmare.

"Ma'am," the other one said, "don't make this any harder on yourself than it has to be."

"Make what any harder? What's going on?" Tessa demanded, willing her voice to remain steady. The last thing she wanted to do in this place was act hysterical – that would be a one-way ticket to the restraint bed.

Her question was met with hard stares. "Stand up and come with us," the one with the deeper voice ordered.

Not wanting to "make things harder" on herself, whatever that meant, she stood. One man on each side of her, they escorted her to a room on a part of the unit she'd never been. The room was stark white with no windows and held nothing but a stained mattress.

"Inside," they ordered.

"What? Why?" Tessa pleaded as she was propelled a few steps forward into the bleak room. "Why are you doing this?" But deep down, she knew why. She was a threat to a monster, and she had to be stopped.

With a loud thump, they pulled the heavy metal door closed behind her. She heard keys rattle. The lock clicked.

She was trapped.

Only the light from the back hall streaming through a small window at the top of the door provided evidence of life outside her isolation. She saw nothing, heard nothing. She was completely alone.

The solitude she'd so desperately wanted when she arrived now came in the form of painted white cinder block walls, a hard tile floor, and a mattress stained by the countless others who'd come before her, finding themselves in this very room, trapped and alone.

87

DREW AND DR. Raymond skipped the elevator and opted to take the stairs up to 3B, where Tessa was being held. Taking them two at a time, they flew up three flights of stairs and, winded but determined to catch her psychiatrist before he left, and arrived at his office door just as he was gathering his things to go home.

They'd made it. Barely.

Startled by their sudden presence, Dr. Armistead said, "Harold, what are you doing here?"

Drew grasped the door frame to steady himself. "You? You're Tessa's psychiatrist? What have you done to her?"

Dr. Raymond leaned against the wall and sucked huge gulps of air into his exhausted lungs. He sputtered, "We... need...to...talk."

Erasing the surprise from his face, Dr. Armistead turned his attention away from the sudden presence of his newly hired financial adviser and focused on his colleague.

"What's the matter?" Dr. Armistead asked as he set his briefcase back on the floor next to his desk.

Drew, recovering more quickly from their sprint up the stairs, demanded, "What have you done to Tessa?"

"Tessa?" Dr. Armistead asked, tapping his chin with his index finger. "If you're talking about Ms. James, she's on the unit." Looking back and forth between Drew and Dr. Raymond, Dr. Armistead said, "Why? What's going on?"

"We know what you've done," Drew accused.

Dr. Raymond held up a hand to cut him off. "Tessa James has been a witness to a crime, and we believe she could be in danger. It's imperative that I speak to her immediately."

Dr. Armistead lowered himself into his chair, then offered the two chairs in front of his desk to Drew and Dr. Raymond. "I'm afraid you won't be able to see her until visiting hours begin at six. Until then, I suggest you take a few laps around the building to cool off," the psychiatrist suggested.

He's stalling. Why? Drew wondered frantically. Has he already done something to her?

"Let me see her," Drew demanded through clenched teeth. "I want to see with my own eyes that she's okay."

"I don't believe Ms. James is in any danger. I saw her just a little while ago," Dr. Armistead protested.

"Tessa saw you! We know what you did!"

"Excuse me? She saw me doing what?" he asked innocently, but the expression on Dr. Armistead's face and the visible constriction of his throat told Drew he knew exactly what Tessa had seen him doing.

88

AS MUCH AS Tessa hated unfamiliar sounds, anything other than the eerie silence would have been welcome. On cue, she heard keys rattle outside the door. Light from the hall filled the room as the door swung open.

Tessa took several cautious steps toward the door, then, realizing who had unlocked it, said, "What was that all about?"

Ann motioned for her to hurry. "Somebody claimed they saw you cheeking your meds. They also said you were becoming confrontational and thought you might get violent."

"I'm not violent," Tessa protested. "I was minding my own business when two Hulks came to throw me in here," she said, waving toward the room behind her.

Ann shrugged. "I don't know, but someone ordered that you be put in seclusion." Her eyes scanned the hall. "I don't think you're safe here." She pointed toward the door at the end of the hall under a glowing red exit sign. "I'm going to open that door. Follow the stairs all the way down. When you get there, you'll be on the bottom floor where we have recovery classes. There are plenty of places to hide but be quick. Nobody knows you're not on the unit. My shift is over in an hour, so sit tight and I'll be there as soon as I can."

"What if I get caught?" Tessa worried aloud. "I don't want to make things worse than they already are."

"You won't get caught," Ann assured her. "Nobody has a reason to be down there at this time of day."

"I don't know…"

"What other choice do you have?" Ann's eyes darkened at the urgency of the situation.

Tessa hesitated. She hated feeling trapped. This must be what Mama felt like all the time, just waiting for the danger lurking in the darkness to come out and destroy her, Tessa thought.

"Okay, I'll go," she said, finally. Ann was right. She had no other choice.

Ann smiled. "Good. Now hurry," She looked over her shoulder and opened the door just wide enough for Tessa to slip through.

As the heavy door snapped shut behind her, she knew she was locked out.

Feet flying down the stairs, Tessa moved quickly through the dimly lit stairwell and opened the door at the very bottom. Ann was right. The entire floor appeared to be abandoned. She tried one door after another, then panicked as she realized they were all locked.

At the far end of the hall, she came to a room with an "Out of order" sign hanging on the door. Whispering a fervent prayer, she twisted the knob.

The door creaked softly as it opened, but in the quiet shadows it might as well have been gunfire. She slipped inside and closed the door behind her, standing completely still until her eyes adjusted to the darkness. The room contained several potter's wheels, and a large kiln stood in the corner.

An hour in this pitch black would stretch on forever, Tessa mused, but it sure beats being stuck behind locked doors with a killer.

Crouching behind the potter's wheel in the farthest corner of the room, she breathed easier knowing somebody would really have to be looking for her to find her there, and the only person who even knew she was down there was Ann.

Ann.

In the darkness, something pricked Tessa's memory. Who would have seen me cheek my meds? There was no one else in the bathroom. It's not possible that anyone could have seen me.

Tessa's heart hammered in her chest. Ann was the one who had suggested cheeking her meds, and Ann was the one who'd said someone saw her.

Could Ann be the one responsible for this?

What do I do now?

As the minutes passed, Tessa noticed a strange odor that became impossible to ignore. It was faint, but it smelled like roadkill. Knees popping as she straightened from a squat, she walked slowly across the room, following the smell until she was standing in front of the kiln.

She took a deep breath, then regretted it. The stench assaulted her. She grasped the handle of the kiln and pulled, the hinges groaning in protest.

Tessa released the handle and covered her mouth and nose with one hand. Using her other to feel her way around the room, she groped the wall for a light switch, flipped it on, and squinted against the sudden brightness.

She turned and took several steps toward the kiln. There,

contorted and stuffed into the small space was the disfigured body of a young woman with dark hair, a bullet hole in the side of her head.

89

AL JEFFERSON'S FEET felt like lead as he puffed his way up the steps.

Had something happened to Tessa James?

There was no question she was in danger, and he felt like a fool for having allowed her to be locked up here. He hadn't realized the man she'd accused of murder worked here.

How had he not known?

The answer was easy. He hadn't cared enough to check.

Still short of breath when he reached unit 3B, he gulped a few more lungfuls of air then banged loudly on the locked steel door.

A man wearing scrubs unlocked it, and Detective Jefferson flashed his badge. "I need to see Tessa James. Now."

"Sure thing. Wait right here, sir," said the man whose name badge read "Dave," then he walked off in the direction of the common room. He then crossed back in front of the nurse's station and walked down another long hall, holding up one finger to indicate it would only take a minute.

His impatience growing, Al watched as Dave walked back

toward the nurse's station, circled around it, and quietly spoke to a female nurse. She walked to the women's bathroom and stuck her head in. She called Tessa's name, then shook her head in Dave's direction when there was no response.

Detective Jefferson saw the female nurse shrug as Dave whispered to her, "Another one is missing?"

An even stronger sense of urgency crept its way up the detective's throat. His gut told him he was too late. Something had already happened to Tessa.

"What's going on?" the detective demanded, not sure he wanted confirmation of what he already suspected.

"I don't exactly know," Dave said nervously. "We can't seem to find Ms. James."

"What do you mean you can't find her? The unit is locked, isn't it? How many places could she be?" Detective Jefferson growled.

Dave turned to face him. "We'll check a few more rooms, but it looks as though Tessa has gone missing."

The words hit Al with the force of an eighteen-wheeler.

Missing? How could she just go missing? And what had Dave meant by "another one?"

"When was the last time anyone saw her?" he demanded, shifting into full interrogation mode.

"Let me gather the staff, and we'll compare notes," Dave offered. "She's got to be around here somewhere. You can't get off the unit without a key."

"Then someone with a key must have let her off," Al muttered.

Several minutes later, the staff was gathered around the nurse's station, each recounting the last time they'd seen Tessa

James. "I just came on duty a little bit ago. I haven't seen her yet," someone said.

"Me either," voiced another.

Finally, a large man who looked to be in his early twenties joined the group. "I put Tessa in seclusion a couple hours ago. When I went to let her out an hour later, she wasn't there. Ann told me Dr. Armistead let her out."

Detective Jefferson's eyes darted around. "Ann? Where is Ann?"

"Her shift was over an hour ago. She's probably on her way home," one of the nursing assistants volunteered.

"Let's fan out and check the whole unit. If we don't find Tessa, we'll have to search the rest of the hospital," Dave said.

The nursing staff took off in opposite directions. Soon after, the sound of slamming doors echoed throughout the unit. As he watched the scrubs-clad staff scurry in every direction, Al considered the likely scenario. He had no doubt there were probably dozens of patients in the hospital with histories of violence. Any one of them could have done something to Tessa, but none of them were as dangerous as the man who'd taken an oath to do no harm.

Fifteen minutes later, the staff gathered again, each shaking their heads. Their mouths formed tight lines across their faces.

"This woman wouldn't just disappear," the detective said. He looked at Dave. "You said 'another one' is missing. What does that mean?"

Dave cleared his throat and began. "We've had a few patients go missing lately. It's weird. That almost never happens."

"We need to find her. Pronto," Detective Jefferson demanded.

Pointing to the two biggest men in the group, Dave said, "You two stay with the patients. The rest of us will look for her off the unit. Detective Jefferson, you come with me."

He followed Dave down the back hall, past the seclusion room. "We'll go out this door and search the stairwells and bottom floor where recovery classes are held. It's empty now, and there are a lot of places to hide."

They walked carefully and quietly down the stairs, eyes scanning each dark corner for any sign of Tessa.

When they reached the door at the bottom of the last flight of stairs, Dave pushed it open and held his finger to his lips "If she's down here, we don't want to scare her," he whispered.

"She's already scared," Al muttered, regret heavy in his words.

Slowly, they made their way down the main corridor, checking behind each door. One by one, they ruled out each classroom as her hiding place.

With a sinking feeling, Al's nearly infallible instinct told him that every moment Tessa remained missing, the lower the likelihood of finding her alive.

90

TESSA SWITCHED THE light off and crouched back into the corner, a new scenario forming in her mind.

Ann was the one who'd told her to cheek her meds. Ann was the one who'd let her out of seclusion and encouraged her to run. It was Ann who'd told her to come down here to hide.

But why was every door other than this one locked? Had somebody taken away her ability to choose her hiding place? Did someone intentionally trap her in this room with a rotting corpse only feet away?

Heart hammering in her chest, Tessa rose to her feet again. She had to escape.

A sound outside the door made her pause and shrink back down. The doorknob turned, the light switched on, and the sound of the deadbolt being snapped shut echoed around the room. Footsteps clicked across the floor, then stopped nearby.

"I'm glad I found you," a voice said.

Tessa peered around the potter's wheel and looked into the face of the man who had set this nightmare into motion. Warning bells rang in her head. *You have to get away!*

"You've made things very difficult for me lately," he said in a chiding voice, addressing her as though she were a child who'd misbehaved. "I've had to deal with a detective snooping around, asking all kinds of questions. Not to mention all the time and energy I've spent tracking you down. You just couldn't leave it alone, could you?" He took another step forward and placed his hand in his pocket. "It didn't have to be this way, you know. If you'd just heeded my warnings, you would have had a long life ahead of you, and that pretty little thing your ex-husband was dating wouldn't be fighting for her life right now." He tilted his head in mock sympathy. "When I'm finished with you, I will make sure she loses that fight. This is all your fault."

A chill raced through her. He was going to try again to kill Camille. And for what? *Because she just happened to show up at my house?*

Mind reeling, Tessa began to pull the pieces together. He'd found her, then lured Camille to her house, only to shoot her? What was the point in that? Tessa wondered.

Keep him talking, her brain urged. *He wants you to know what he's done.*

"I wouldn't ever intend to cause trouble for you," she said, forcing her voice to sound calm. "But that woman needed me."

Dr. Armistead grunted. "Margo? She didn't need anybody. She made that perfectly clear. If you hadn't been sticking your nose where it didn't belong, nobody would have missed her."

"Everybody needs somebody. She must have just been confused. Sometimes we want to be able to make it on our own. We convince ourselves we don't need anybody, but that's not true," Tessa continued, the irony of her words striking her own heart.

"I loved her," the doctor protested. "I loved her, and she pushed me away. I couldn't let her get away with that."

"It must have been difficult for you to have your love thrown back in your face. That wasn't fair to you."

"No, it wasn't," he agreed. "It also wasn't fair of you to keep after the police to harass me. I'm a good person; I have helped so many sick people. You're trying to take all that away."

"I'm sure you have been very helpful to your patients. It's not right to hurt people, though," Tessa said gently.

The psychiatrist snorted, obviously disgusted with Tessa's assessment of his actions. "You're just like your mother. She tried to make things hard for me, too." He smirked. "We know how that worked out or her."

Tessa's mouth went dry. She tried to swallow around the sudden lump in her throat. "My mother?"

"She was a feisty one. Just like you. Also like you, she suspected I didn't have my patients' best interest at heart."

"You knew my mother," Tessa said, the words sounding like they were coming from someone else.

He nodded and slowly pulled his hand from his pocket, a long syringe clutched in his palm. "She wanted to get better. She wanted a better life, so she came to see me." His mouth drooped in a mocking frown. "Too bad it didn't work out the way she'd hoped."

"I saw you," Tessa murmured. "You're the one I saw running through her backyard."

"Lucky for me, nobody believed you. You even doubted yourself. I'm guessing you even began to wonder if you were turning into dear old mother."

Fresh hatred for this man rose in her chest. Mama had

been trying to get better, was getting help, and this monster had taken away her chance.

Tessa rose on wobbly legs. "Why? Why did you have to kill my mom? What could she have possibly done to deserve being murdered?"

Jacob Armistead shifted the syringe in his hand and pulled the plastic cap off the needle. "I don't want to talk anymore. I think I've been more than generous by letting you know what happened to your dearly departed mother before you die."

Slipping the cap back into his pocket, he shifted his thumb to the plunger and took one last step toward Tessa, stopping mere inches from her. He raised the syringe and narrowed his eyes. "Looks like you're going to end up like her after all."

91

DETECTIVE ISAAC DUNN made record time getting back to the hospital. He'd only been at the station a few minutes when Al had called to let him know Tessa was missing.

Now, after a quick stop by the hospital receptionist's desk for directions, his shoes were thudding on the hard tile floor. At the far end of the corridor on the lowest level of the hospital, a group was gathered outside a door as a man in scrubs fumbled with his keys.

"Hurry up!" Al demanded.

Finally, the man inserted his keys into the lock and pushed the door open. Dr. Jacob Armistead's back was to them, a long syringe in his hand. His thumb was on the plunger, ready to strike.

Isaac moved ahead of the group and lunged forward, in tandem with Al, throwing their bodies on top of the doctor's. The sound of air whooshing out of Jacob Armistead's lungs filled the room as the trio tumbled to the floor. The syringe clattered onto the floor next to them.

Wiggling an arm free from Detective Dunn's grip, the

psychiatrist grabbed the syringe, held it high, and plunged it into his own neck. His face distorted in a mask of rage, he screeched, "I am the master of my destiny, and you won't take me to jail!" With that, his neck relaxed and his head dropped to the side. His body convulsed, then went still.

His eyes wide and staring, a maniacal smile frozen on his face, Dr. Jacob Armistead would finally keep his oath to do no harm.

92

TESSA ROSE ON unsteady legs from where she'd fallen in her attempt to get away from the detectives tackling her would-be killer. She brushed herself off with shaky hands, and croaked, "Detectives?"

They turned away from Jacob Armistead's lifeless body to face her.

"The woman I saw him carrying is over there," she said, pointing toward the kiln.

Detective Jefferson nodded and walked toward it, opened the door, and shuddered. The stench of rotting corpse filled the room. He pulled his phone from his pocket and punched in the numbers of the police station. "We need the crime scene techs to get down here right away. We've a couple of bodies here."

Disconnecting the call, the detective looked back toward Tessa. "I'll need you to come to the station to answer some questions about what happened here tonight."

Tessa nodded and sighed. "It sounds better than being in this place."

A moment later, Detective Jefferson was back on the

phone, this time with Judge Cooper, requesting that Tessa be let out of the hospital early. He also asked for a warrant to search Dr. Armistead's home and office. His demeanor when he disconnected the call spoke volumes to Tessa. She'd be getting out of here, even if it was just long enough to go to the police station.

An hour later, flanked by her rescuers, Tessa entered the station. She smiled broadly, never imagining it would feel so good to be there. They stopped at Detective Jefferson's desk, where he bent over and began shuffling through some papers.

She'd give her statement, and then, as long as the judge agreed, she would hopefully be allowed to go home on her own recognizance. There was nowhere she'd rather be than home, secure in the knowledge that she was safe, that monster out of her life forever.

Tessa turned at the sound of footsteps to see Drew standing behind her. With a wry smile, she said, "You didn't come visit me at the hospital."

Drew bent over and wrapped his arms around her. "I'm never letting you out of my sight again," he whispered into her hair. "Now we just have to get you cleared of shooting Camille, and you'll be home free."

"Free," Tessa repeated softly. When was the last time she really felt free?

As she recounted the events of the evening, Detective Jefferson nodded and took notes, interjecting a question here and there. Drew sat beside her, tightly holding her hand like he had every intention of keeping his promise.

When she was finished talking, the detective nodded his head and laid his pen on the desk. "I've got one more call to make," he said, picking up his phone.

Tessa's hope soared as she listened to the detective request that she not be placed back in jail while they worked to get the details of the case ironed out. He paused, then looked at Tessa while still speaking to the judge. "Yes, I'm sure she would be more than happy to wear a tracking device."

Nodding vigorously, Tessa said, "Whatever it takes, I'll do it."

"Thank you, sir," Detective Jefferson said, then dropped the phone back in its cradle. He turned his attention to Tessa. "As long as you agree to abide by some rules, it looks like you'll be sleeping in your own bed tonight."

93

WITH A TRACKING device strapped around her ankle, Tessa walked through the front door of the police station and out into the fresh night air, Drew at her side.

Dr. Raymond sat on the steps and rose as she approached. "I'm so sorry," he said, shaking his head. "I didn't know it would turn out like this."

Tessa shook her head. "There's no way you could have known. But I'm okay. A killer has been taken off the streets, and I finally know what happened to Mama."

At the puzzled looks on the faces of Drew and Dr. Raymond, she explained Dr. Armistead's confession that he'd been treating her mother, and when she became suspicious of his activities, he'd killed her.

"I wasn't imagining things when I said I saw a man running through her yard. It was him." Tessa closed her eyes and took a deep breath. "I guess I didn't end up like Mama after all." She paused. "She was braver than I ever gave her credit for. I assumed she was too sick to realize she needed help. She knew, though, and she wanted to get better." A tear rolled down Tessa's cheek. "Anita Wells, I hereby release you from the blame of screwing me up beyond repair."

"Who?" Dr. Raymond asked.

"Mama. Her name was Anita Wells."

The psychologist snapped his fingers. "That's why you look so familiar," he said, then in response to the questioning glances, he continued. "When the ink on my doctoral degree was still wet, I did my post-doctoral work at the old psychiatric hospital. I had a patient named Anita Wells. She was a very smart, very scared young woman. The first time you came to see me, I thought your eyes looked familiar. Now I know why." He smiled. "You've got your mother's eyes."

"I do," Tessa agreed, "and that's not all I got from her." She smiled. The weight of the responsibility she'd put on herself to care for her mom, and the self-blame for failing her was finally lifted from her shoulders. She hadn't failed her. Mama had been a survivor.

Just like Tessa.

Epilogue

One Week Later

TESSA PULLED THE story she'd just written off the printer and gave it a quick once-over. She'd taken a chance in asking Jack if she could write the inside scoop about what had gone on last week, and he'd hesitantly agreed. The story had already been covered by other news outlets, but none of them had the perspective of someone who lived through it. Though difficult to write, Tessa was proud of the end result.

The story covered Dr. Jacob Armistead's string of murders, which dated back more than a decade, as well as the attempted murders of Camille Walker and Tessa James. She'd also mentioned his intent to go back to Camille's hospital room and ensure she could never identify him as her shooter. His choice to commit suicide rather than be taken into custody was also included.

Dr. Armistead had kept a detailed journal that described the murders of Margo Lang, Amanda Meyers, and Anita Wells. He'd listed many others as well, and Tessa was proud to have played a part in bringing closure to the families of the other victims.

Dr. Armistead's accomplice, Ann Mason, was found stabbed

to death in her car. Though there was no entry in the journal about her murder, it was assumed he was responsible.

She ended the story with Camille Walker's ongoing recovery and, for the sake of human interest, included her budding romance with one of the male nurses she'd met in the ICU.

Tucked deep in the story was a call for society to increase its awareness of mental illness. She'd learned firsthand that there were a lot of people with misconceptions about those struggling with psychiatric disorders. She remembered Martha's comment about the revolving door and wondered who was occupying the bed she'd slept in only a week ago. Thoughts of Mama still haunted her. Mama, who'd finally recognized her need for help had been silenced.

Tessa would be her voice.

Laying the page on the desk, Tessa was satisfied that she'd told the story in a way that would honor the victims and their families. She opened her email and attached the file, then pressed send.

Her work there was done.

A knock at the front door pulled her from her thoughts. When she opened it, she was surprised to see Detective Jefferson standing there.

He looked down at his shoes and said, "I just wanted to tell you I'm sorry. I'm sorry you were ever put in that kind of danger, and I'm sorry I stopped believing you. I hope you can forgive me."

Tessa smiled and reached for the detective's hand. Giving it a squeeze, she said, "All is forgiven. Thank you for rescuing me."

Detective Jefferson dropped his eyes to the floor. "When I found out your mom was sick, I guess I assumed some of that rubbed off on you."

"I see," Tessa said softly, a knot forming in her stomach. Another misconception.

Shuffling his feet, he said, "My little sister was murdered twenty years ago by a man who'd developed a fixation on her. She was only nineteen, a sophomore in college, and was walking back to her dorm room after a meeting with her academic advisor. The guy was schizophrenic, had been in and out of hospitals for years, and had a history of violent behavior." The detective's eyes watered. "She never saw him coming. Ever since then, I've been extra vigilant when one of my witnesses has a family history of mental illness. I'm sorry to say, I was skeptical of everything you told me."

"I understand. I only hope that I've helped you see that your doubts aren't always justified."

"Yes, you have. It seems that I have a lot to learn." The detective smiled, then grew serious. "We got the results back from the good doctor's tox screen. It looks like he was intending to inject you with cyanide."

A shiver raced down Tessa's spine. If they hadn't gotten there when they did, she would have been dead long before anyone found her.

Detective Jefferson cleared his throat. "Well, I wish you all the best. Take care of yourself," he said, then turned and walked back to his car.

"You, too," Tessa replied as the detective opened his car door.

Tessa had survived the darkest hours of her life, and was, for the first time in her memory, confident she could face whatever happened next.

Note from the Author

This story exists because I couldn't get the line *Mama taught me monsters are real* out of my head. What if the story revolved around a woman who was raised by a paranoid mother? How would her childhood affect her life as an adult? What would be her biggest fear? I grew to love Tessa James, and hope I communicated her strength and vulnerability in a way that made you love her, too.

I have been fascinated by mental illness for more than two decades, which would explain my undergraduate and graduate degrees. After college, my first job in the mental health field was at a state psychiatric hospital. Many of the events that take place in the hospital scenes are inspired by my work at the hospital.

If you suffer with mental illness and have yet to seek help, know that you aren't alone and that there is no shame in needing support. Speak up and speak out. You can help destigmatize mental illness.

National Suicide Prevention Lifeline: 1-800-273-8255
www.suicidepreventionlifeline.org

National Alliance on Mental Illness: 1-800-950-6264
www.nami.org

Acknowledgements

Once again, I'm reminded that it takes a village to take a story from an idea and rough draft to a finished product that is worthy of being placed in a reader's hands.

To my editors, Stephen Parolini and Caroline Knecht, who helped smooth the rough edges of this story. Thank you for the encouraging comments and the learning experience.

The designers at Damonza, who have a knack for creating beautiful books, inside and out.

To my husband, Billy, who has always encouraged me to do what I love, as well as many friends and family who continue to spur me on with their support. I love you all!

Finally, to you, the reader. A story doesn't come alive until it's in your hands. I hope you have enjoyed reading this story as much as I enjoyed writing it.

Until next time!
Erin

www.ingramcontent.com/pod-product-compliance
Lightning Source LLC
Chambersburg PA
CBHW031622100726
47898CB00006B/1912